The Hardy Boys
in
The Secret of the Caves

The Hardy Boys Mystery Stories

The Secret of the Caves

Franklin W. Dixon

Armada

First published in the U.K. in 1972 by
William Collins Sons & Co. Ltd., London and Glasgow.
First published in Armada in 1977 by
Fontana Paperbacks,
14 St. James's Place, London SW1A 1PS.

This impression 1980.

Printed in Great Britain by
Love & Malcomson Ltd., Brighton Road,
Redhill, Surrey.

CONTENTS

Frank leaped towards the ledge and grabbed the shotgun.

·1·

Telescope Hill Trouble

"DON'T kid me, fellows," chubby Chet Morton said, moving his metal detector about the Hardys' front lawn. "You can find all kinds of things on the beaches with this gadget."

"Like what?" blond-haired Joe asked, winking at his brother Frank.

"Lost jewellery, money, gold-plated pens—"

Chet was interrupted by the arrival of a tall, broad-shouldered youth.

"Hi, Biff!" Frank called out. "Chet's trying to find a treasure."

Biff Hooper examined the new device and raised his eyebrows. "I know just where you can use this, Chet. You might find a lot of valuable stuff."

"Where?"

"At the Honeycomb Caves. My grandfather told me a freighter was sunk off the point during a hurricane. Lots of stuff was washed up."

"Just what I told you," Chet said, with a supercilious glance at the Hardy brothers.

Frank, eighteen, and Joe, a year younger, looked sceptically at their enthusiastic friends.

"There are a lot of important things to be found!"

Chet burbled. "How about the four of us going on a trip together?"

"To the Honeycomb Caves?" Joe asked.

"Sure. Why not? It's only fifty miles down the coast. Good swimming and fishing there, too."

"I'll explore the caves for hidden jewels," Joe said dryly, "while you and Biff pick up a million dollars' worth of rusty nails."

"It's a deal," Biff said, laughing. "Let me try that gimmick, Chet."

The stout boy removed the earphones from his head and handed Biff the long thin tube with a metal disc at the end.

"When you hear a loud clicking," Chet said, "you know that something metallic is under the ground."

His face intent, big Biff moved about the grass with the detector. Suddenly a voice from inside the house called, "Frank! Joe!"

"Okay, Dad, we're coming," Joe answered. He leaped up the front steps three at a time, with Frank at his heels.

Inside, Mr Hardy, a tall athletic man, motioned his sons into his study.

Fenton Hardy's reputation as a sleuth was world-wide. A former crack New York City police officer, he had moved to Bayport to become a private detective. Now his sons seemed destined to follow in their father's footsteps.

"What's cooking, Dad?" Frank asked, as the two boys sank into comfortable seats.

"Another mystery?" queried Joe.

Mr Hardy flashed a smile, then became serious and

opened a dossier before him on the desk. "I've got important news," he said.

"About what, Dad?" Joe asked.

"Telescope Hill."

"Where the U.S. is erecting the Coastal Radar Station?" asked Frank.

"Exactly."

"What's going on there?" Joe asked.

"Trouble. That's all I know so far," Mr Hardy replied. He told his sons that he had been deputized by the U.S. Government to aid in security at the gigantic installation designed to protect the coast of North America.

"To hunt out spies?" Joe asked.

"More likely saboteurs. There have been some strange, unexplained accidents at the site."

"Attack from within?" Frank queried.

"Yes. Perhaps a guard. That's my guess. I'm going to reorganize the guard security system and nip trouble in the bud. I thought you boys might like to help."

"Sure, Dad!" Frank said. "Will we need disguises or anything?"

"Not exactly."

"But," Joe began, "Chet wants us to—"

"That can wait," Frank interrupted impatiently. "Can't you see, Joe, we might be heading into a dilly of a mystery?"

Just then the quiet of the balmy June afternoon was shattered by a wild shriek in front of the Hardys' home. Frank and Joe jumped up, startled.

"Good grief, something's happened!" Frank exclaimed.

Both boys dashed out of the house, followed by Mr Hardy. Chet was jumping up and down on the front lawn, while Biff, looking excited, made the metal disc hover above a spot on the lawn.

"He's found a treasure!" Chet cried out. "This thing's clicking like fury. We've really got something, Frank!"

Several cars passing the Hardy home slowed down as the drivers watched Chet's antics. Then a huge trailer truck, carrying a load of construction steel, came to a halt while the driver honked for the cars to move on.

"More material for the radar installation," Frank thought, as the long vehicle rumbled out of sight down the street.

"Look, it's just about here," Biff said. He took off his earphones and marked an X on the grass.

"Do you expect us to dig up this fine lawn to satisfy your tomfoolery?" Joe said in mock seriousness.

"We just can't let it lie there," Chet protested. "Suppose it's an old coin worth hundreds and hundreds of dollars."

Now Mr Hardy was interested. With a wink he said, "Okay, boys, dig it up. Let's see what good detectives Chet and Biff are."

Chet ran to the garage and returned with a spade. With it he carefully cut the turf, placed it to one side, and probed the dirt with the point of his spade. He hit something hard and metallic.

"What did I tell you?" Chet beamed. "This detector is the greatest. Oh boy, are we going to have fun at Honeycomb Caves!" He dug up a spadeful of dirt, which he deposited beside the hole.

From the soil fell the metallic object. The Hardys recognized it as a tiny toy fire engine, rusted and corroded.

As the others crowded about, Joe picked up the toy and wiped off the crumbling earth which clung to the wheels. "Thanks, Chet," he said gravely, "I lost this fire engine seven years ago when I was ten."

"You were probably trying to hide it from me," said Frank, and laughed.

"Well," said Biff, "we've found Chet's Number One treasure. What's next? A ship's compass at Honeycomb Caves?"

Chuckling, Mr Hardy excused himself, while the boys chatted about the trip.

"I'm afraid we can't go, fellows," Joe said.

"Not this time, anyhow," Frank chimed in. "We have to work on a case with Dad."

"Say, what is going on?" Biff demanded.

"We can't tell," Frank replied. "It's confidential."

"Whatever it is," Chet said, "count me out of any dangerous stuff." Their stout friend bemoaned the fact that every time they were about to have fun, some sort of detective work had to come up.

Chet already had been involved in some deep mysteries which the Hardy boys had solved. But in each case, although reluctant at first, their staunch friend had joined in the sleuthing as an invaluable ally.

"When can you come with us?" asked Biff, evidently as eager as Chet to explore around Honeycomb Caves.

"That depends," said Frank, "on—" His eyes were suddenly diverted by someone walking up the street. The other three boys turned to see an attractive girl about their age hurrying along the pavement. She had wavy jet black hair, flashing brown eyes, and a gait that told the world she was in a hurry.

"A new neighbour?" Biff whispered, grinning.

"I've never seen her before," Joe said.

The girl, heels clicking, hastened to the Hardys' front path. There she stopped suddenly, turned towards the boys, and took a few steps forward.

Chet gave a low whistle and rolled his eyes. The girl, although she had a pretty face, wore a sad, worried look. "I would like to speak to the detective," she said nervously.

Joe's face brightened. "My brother Frank and I are detectives," he replied. "May we help you?"

"Don't mock me," said the girl, and her lower lip quivered.

Frank and Joe were taken aback. But they were even more nonplussed when their caller suddenly burst into tears!

·2·

Over the Fence

"HEY, wait a minute!" Joe blurted. "Don't cry!" But tears continued to course down the girl's face.

As the boys looked on in embarrassed silence, Mrs Hardy hurried out of the door, followed by her husband.

"Goodness gracious!" exclaimed Laura Hardy, a slim, good-looking woman. She hastened to the girl and put an arm about her shoulder. "Come inside, dear. Perhaps we can help you."

Frank whispered to Chet and Biff, "Wait here until we find out what this is all about."

Mrs Hardy sat on the living-room sofa beside the young caller. The girl dried her eyes and announced that her name was Mary Todd. She sobbed once more and said, "My father was a friend of yours, Mr Hardy."

"Oh, yes. George Todd of the Redding Machine Company. A fine man. I haven't seen him for years."

"Well, Dad passed away, and Mother too," the girl said.

The Hardys all expressed sympathy. Then Mary explained, "That's not why I'm crying, though. It's about my brother."

Mr Hardy leaned forward in his chair and said, "His

name is Morgan, isn't it? As I recall, a very bright boy. A little older than my sons."

Bravely fighting back tears, Mary told the Hardys that her brother, Morgan Thomas Todd, an instructor on foreign affairs at Kenworthy College, had disappeared.

"And I want you to find him, Mr Hardy," Mary said pleadingly. "The police are working on the case, but have discovered no leads."

The girl explained that she was a freshman at Kenworthy College, which had just ended the spring term. Her plan had been to spend the summer with relatives on the West Coast, but since her brother had disappeared several days before, she had cancelled her trip and come to Bayport.

"I just don't know what to do, Mr Hardy," she said. "Please help me."

Frank and Joe looked at their father. What would his decision be? He thought for a moment before speaking. "As I recall, your brother spent some time studying political methods in a foreign country."

"Yes, he did," Mary said, and mentioned the nation, which was unfriendly to the United States. She added that while he was there, Morgan Todd had suffered a fall and injured his head. "He seemed all right when he came back, but now I'm afraid he's lost his memory and just wandered away from the college."

"You mean as the result of his fall?" Mrs Hardy asked.

"Yes. A sort of delayed reaction."

"Fenton, I hope you take the case," Mrs Hardy said earnestly.

The detective now gave Mary a reassuring smile. "Of course I will." He turned to Frank and Joe. "You know I have already accepted an important case, but if you boys pitch in, I can also undertake the search for Morgan."

"Dad, you know we will!" Joe said eagerly.

Mary Todd's face brightened. "Oh, thank you, thank you," she said. "Boys, please forgive me for being such a crybaby."

"That's all right," Joe replied, a little embarrassed.

"Sure," Frank put in. "I don't blame you. Maybe we acted a little too smart. Have you a picture of your brother?" he added.

Mary took a snapshot from her purse and gave it to Frank. "Just don't lose it," she said, smiling. Then she rose to bid them good-bye. "I'll be staying at the Bayport Hotel," she said.

At that moment the doorbell rang. Mrs Hardy answered it and an attractive dark-haired girl walked in. She was Iola Morton, Chet's sister, who was a schoolmate of the Hardys and a particular favourite of Joe's.

"Hello, Iola," Joe said, reddening slightly.

Then Frank said, "Iola, this is Mary Todd."

The two girls smiled and exchanged greetings. Then Iola said, "Joe, what did you and Frank do to my poor brother? He's simply crushed that you two won't go treasure-hunting at Honeycomb Caves."

"You can guess what the reason is," Frank said.

Iola giggled. "A mystery?"

Frank and Joe, after a nod of approval from their father, told her about Mary Todd's problem.

"Oh, you poor dear," Iola said kindly. Her eyes sparkled. "I have an idea! Suppose you stay at our home until Mr Hardy and the boys find your brother."

"Oh, I couldn't impose."

"You don't know my mother," Iola said. "She'll insist that you stay. I hope you don't mind being a little way out in the country. We live on a farm."

"I'd really love it," Mary said. "You're all so wonderful to me."

The two girls left the house together. Frank and Joe followed and quickly briefed Chet and Biff on the missing instructor.

"Another mystery! That settles it!" Chet exclaimed. He turned to the Hardys and said gravely, "Gentlemen, the Hooper-Morton treasure expedition will be forced to take off without you."

"Come on, Chet," Iola ordered. "Get that old jalopy of yours running, destination Bayport Hotel."

"What for?" her brother asked, putting his metal detector in the back of the car.

When Iola told about their new guest, Chet opened the door gallantly with a bow. "The two of you can squeeze into the front seat with me," he said, then gave Biff a big wink and murmured, "Some guys have all the luck."

"That's you, pal." Biff laughed.

At the dinner-table that evening Frank and Joe discussed with their father what steps to take first in both mysteries. The brothers, it was decided, would leave the next day for Kenworthy College, in upper New York State. It was located in a town of the same name, about a six-hour drive away.

"And now getting back to my case at the radar site," Mr Hardy said, "I'll show you around the place tonight."

"Great!" Joe exclaimed eagerly.

Ever since the brothers had been old enough to engage in sleuthing, there had been a great camaraderie among the Hardy "menfolk," as Laura Hardy referred to them. Frank and Joe had first demonstrated their detective ability in an adventure known as *The Mystery of the Aztec Warrior*. Their most recent challenge was *The Wailing Siren Mystery*. By now, crime detection had become the boys' chief avocation.

The three left the house and Frank backed the boys' car down the driveway. The vehicle was old but well kept by the brothers, who preferred it to their father's new sedan.

Frank drove five miles north of the town to an elevated spot overlooking the Atlantic Ocean, and directly below, Barmet Bay.

From the road they could see Bayport hugging the coast, with its many docks stretching like dark fingers into the bay. Frank drove for half a mile farther. Now the road was bordered by a high steel-mesh fence. Presently he stopped in front of a gate guarded by two uniformed men. Mr Hardy got out and showed his badge, then introduced his sons to the guards. "I'd like to show the boys around," he said.

"Okay, Mr Hardy," one of the guards replied, saluting.

The three Hardys tramped along a wooded lane which snaked upwards to the top of Telescope Hill.

"Little did the old pioneers know that their telescope

lookout would be used for this giant radar,'' Frank said, as they approached the summit.

Here the trees had been felled, and the area was covered with heavy construction equipment and piles of steel framework. Already the radar tower had risen more than a hundred feet into the air, its girders sticking up weirdly into the evening sky.

"Looks like nobody's around," Joe said, glancing about. "Sure is quiet."

"Don't be fooled," Mr Hardy told him. "There's a large corps of watchmen on duty."

"Still, it's a pretty big place to be patrolled one hundred per cent efficiently, isn't it, Dad?" Joe asked.

"You're right."

Just then another uniformed guard walked quietly past the construction equipment twenty yards from them. "Evening, Mr Hardy," the man said.

"Evening, Bill." Fenton Hardy returned his salute, then walked on with his sons. They encountered three more guards before they had circled the hilltop.

Each man was immediately recognized by the detective, although he had met the entire staff only that morning.

On the way back to the gate, Frank left the lane. Walking waist-high through weeds and brush, he observed the fence. "I wonder if they're planning to electrify the fence?" he called out to his father.

Before Mr Hardy could answer, Frank was startled by rustling noises. A dim figure rose up from the brush about ten feet away. Stealthily as a cat, a man raced to the fence.

"Stop!" Frank yelled, and sprinted after him. The

fellow clawed his way to the top of the steel mesh and leaped down with the agility of a panther. He hit the ground with a thud on the other side and bounded off into the woods. Mr Hardy and Joe dashed to Frank's side.

"Jumpin' catfish!" Joe declared. "You've already flushed one of the spy pack."

"I hope not for good," Frank said. "I'd rather have grabbed him."

Suddenly his eye was caught by an object snagged on a bush. Frank plucked it off and triumphantly held out an odd-looking cap. "We've got a clue, anyhow."

The trio examined the cap. It was dark red with a small green peak. There was no label inside.

"I've never seen one like this," Joe commented. "It could be an import."

"Good guess," Frank agreed.

It was growing dark, so Mr Hardy voted against pursuing the intruder. He kept the cap, however, for more careful study.

Next morning Frank and Joe were up early. They hastily packed for the trip to Kenworthy College, then had breakfast with their parents.

"You have a plan mapped out, boys?" Mr Hardy asked.

Frank nodded and laid down his fork. "We'll see the police and the dean, then get permission to examine Morgan Todd's quarters."

"Check carefully on any close associates he might have had," Mr Hardy advised.

"And do be careful," Mrs Hardy added. "Of course,

I know you're perfectly capable of taking care of your-selves."

"You can say that again, Laura," Mr Hardy re-marked as a smile crinkled his eyes.

Joe checked the petrol and oil in their car while Frank loaded the luggage into the boot. "All set."

"Okay." Joe took the wheel and zigzagged through the Bayport streets until they came to the highway which led directly west. Early morning traffic was light, consisting mainly of large trucks heading east towards the radar construction.

The road, level at first, rose in a long curve towards the top of a hill, three miles out of town.

Joe kept far to the right side as a truck crested the hill and headed down. It was pulling a long trailer, on top of which was balanced a huge crane.

As it approached, Frank suddenly cried out, "Joe . . . the trailer . . . it's cut loose!"

The trailer veered towards the centre of the road on a collision course with the Hardys' car.

Joe tried desperately to swerve out of its way. To make matters worse, the huge crane began to topple over.

"Look out!" Frank cried in warning.

·3·

Bouncy Quill

FRANTICALLY Joe looked about for a way to dodge the runaway trailer. He spied a small lay-by and spun his wheel sharply. But before he could reach that haven, the crane hit the top of the Hardys' car with a ripping crash!

Joe clutched the wheel as the car swerved and shuddered, finally coming to rest on the dirt shoulder. Both boys glanced back. The huge crane lay twisted in a ditch, the trailer alongside on its back. Frank and Joe hopped out to look at the damage.

"Wow! Look at this. Pretty close!" Frank said, pointing to a long jagged cut in the roof of the car.

A quarter of a mile down the hill, the truck driver had stopped his vehicle and walked back. He came up to the Hardys and the three talked over the strange accident. As they surveyed the broken crane and the trailer with upturned wheels still spinning, the truck driver said glumly, "More bad luck. We're really getting it on this radar job!"

"What do you mean?" Frank asked. "Have things like this happened before?"

The driver hooked his thumbs into his braces and gave a low whistle. "Happened before! I'll say!" He told the boys that in three days this was the third accident to heavy equipment bound for the radar project.

"So now I've got to make out more papers and reports for the construction company," the driver said, as if this were even more difficult than driving his unwieldy rig.

Joe took out his wallet. "We have to report to our insurance company," he said. "They'll take care of everything."

After Joe and the driver had exchanged information, the boys set off again. As they drove along the highway, the Hardys speculated on the unusual accident. Was this a case of sabotage? Did it have anything to do with their father's assignment, or the intruder they had seen the night before?

"I don't see how it could have been aimed at us personally," Joe said.

"I agree," his brother replied. "Could've been a weak coupling. Or perhaps the trailer brakes didn't hold. The claims investigators will find out."

The brothers stopped for a quick lunch along the way, and arrived at the outskirts of Kenworthy an hour later with Frank at the wheel.

"Keep an eye open for a place to stay," he said as he reduced speed.

They passed several motels, none of which looked particularly inviting.

"Hey, Frank, what about that place ahead?" Joe suggested. A large billboard announced that the Palm Court Motel offered the traveller the latest luxuries.

"Not a bad-looking place." Frank pulled into a

driveway which led to a cottage with a simulated thatched roof. It bore the sign OFFICE. To the left stretched a long, low building made up of the motel units. Before each door stood an artificial palm tree. Frank and Joe got out and looked around. To the right of the office they counted twelve neat little cottages of the same thatched-roof variety. The ubiquitous palm tree stood before each one.

"Kind of corny," Joe remarked.

"But comfortable looking," his brother said. "We might do worse."

In the office they were greeted by a middle-aged man with a thin fringe of hair circling his head an inch above the ears. He stroked his bald head and greeted the boys with a smile. "College students visiting from somewhere else?"

Frank evaded the question and asked the price of a motel room. When he was told, Frank registered for himself and his brother, took the proffered key, then drove the car in front of Unit Seven.

As the boys entered with their luggage, Joe grinned. "Some people are pretty nosey."

"The less people know about our business the better," Frank said, as he put his suitcase on a rack, then opened it.

After they had refreshed themselves, the boys went out, locked the door, and hopped into the car.

"First port of call," Frank said, "will be the police station."

"Good idea." Joe nodded. "Let's learn what the local cops found out."

Police headquarters was in the basement of the newly-built town hall. The chief was out of town, so the boys introduced themselves to the desk sergeant and asked for background regarding the Todd case.

"Morgan Todd just walked out and disappeared," said the sergeant. "Absent-minded professor kind of stuff, you know."

"Any clues at all?" Joe asked.

"Nope, nothing," the sergeant replied. "But we'll probably hear from him in a few days." He leaned forward. "Confidentially, I think he was one of these overworked eggheads. You know, studying all the time. Too much strain!"

The boys did not comment, but thanked the officer and left.

"Talk about jumping to conclusions!" said Joe, when they were in the car again. "That sergeant takes the biscuit!"

They decided next to talk with the dean.

After getting directions from a passerby, Frank drove to the outskirts of town, where the small college nestled on a wooded knoll. Frank stopped in front of the administration building. He and Joe climbed the marble steps and entered the hallway.

They quickly found the office marked DEAN EAST-LAND, and went inside. After telling a receptionist that the nature of their business was confidential, the Hardys were ushered into the official's private office.

Dean Eastland was a tall, spare man with a shock of unruly grey hair. He rose as they entered. "Be seated, young men. You say your mission is confidential? That sounds mysterious."

The brothers took chairs before the dean's desk, and

Frank began by saying that they were trying to find Morgan Todd.

"Yes, yes, good for you," the dean said. "Matter of fact, we're all trying to locate him."

"Our father, Fenton Hardy, has taken on the case," Frank explained, "and we are here to do a little spadework."

"Ah, yes, yes. I hope you have better luck than we have had," the college official said. "Strange! Very strange indeed!" He shook his head.

"How's that?" Frank asked.

"Well, I mean, the circumstances surrounding his departure." As the boys listened intently, Dean Eastland told how the instructor apparently had prepared an examination for his students, left it on his desk, and disappeared into the night.

"We found the test there next morning," the dean said, "or rather a colleague found it, had it mimeographed, and Mr Todd's students took the examination that day."

The dean picked up a pencil and tapped it on his desk. "But, as you know, Mr Todd never returned. Quite disturbing."

"Who found the exam?" Joe asked impetuously.

The dean looked up in surprise. "Mr Quill did. Cadmus Quill is Mr Todd's colleague and close associate."

Frank and Joe exchanged meaningful glances. They would have to question Cadmus Quill.

"Well, that is about as much as I can tell you, boys," said the dean, rising. "Morgan Todd, I'm afraid, is suffering from loss of memory."

"We'd like to meet Cadmus Quill," Frank said, "and also examine Todd's room if we may, Dean Eastland."

The dean jotted down the address and handed Frank the slip of paper. He walked to the window and pointed across the quadrangle. "Shelly Row is behind that building. It's where we house graduate students and instructors."

The boys thanked the dean and hurried out. As they walked across the quadrangle, they passed groups of students who had just registered for the summer session.

Presently the brothers found themselves behind a short man in his early twenties, noticeable because of his tiptoed bouncy gait and a loud sports jacket. Joe could hardly keep from imitating the peculiar walk as he fell in behind him.

Frank nudged his brother, and as they stepped past the man, Joe could not restrain himself from taking a backward glance at the fellow's intelligent, round face.

Quickly finding Shelly Row, the boys made their way to Number 19 and rang the doorbell. They were so intent on listening for someone inside that they did not hear a person walking up behind them. "Looking for me?" asked a cheerful voice.

Frank and Joe whirled about to face the bouncy fellow with the sporty clothes. "Are you Cadmus Quill?" Frank asked.

"Yes, I am. May I help you?"

The boys introduced themselves, and Quill ushered them into his room. Frank quickly told all that they had learned about the case and asked Quill if he knew anything further.

"I do indeed," he replied, "but the local police think it isn't important!"

"Do you have more facts?" Joe asked eagerly.

"Not exactly," Quill replied. "You might say it's confidential information." He motioned the boys to be seated, then drew up a chair close to them. "Todd was going to be married soon. Did you know that?"

Taken by surprise, the Hardys said No.

Quill told them that Todd had confided in him that he was going to return to Europe to marry a girl he had met while studying in the unfriendly country. "He didn't even tell his sister for fear she might object."

"Then you don't believe he lost his memory," Frank said.

Quill shook his head. "Not at all."

The graduate assistant had no further information to offer, whereupon the Hardys asked if he would show them to Todd's quarters.

"Indeed," Quill said with an officious little smile. "Right next door."

He produced a key and entered the adjoining apartment.

"You see? Everything is neat and orderly," he pointed out. "It's very obvious to me that Morgan deliberately planned to leave."

"What's this?" Frank asked, bending down to look at some mimeographed sheets on Todd's desk.

"I put those there," Quill replied, "—a few of the examination papers which were left over the day after Morgan disappeared."

The young sleuths scanned the room but did not wish to examine it closely with Quill present.

"Thank you," Frank said. "Guess that's all for now. May we come back later and check the room further?"

"Indeed, yes, be my guests," Quill said, and he handed the key to Joe.

As they returned to their car, Frank teased his brother. "Joe, you nearly made a *faux pas* when we first saw Bouncy Quill walking across the campus."

Joe laughed. "He's kind of odd, but I suppose a very smart cooky."

The boys stopped for supper at an inn near the campus, then returned to their motel. Frank opened the door and gasped. Inside was an elderly couple. The man was reading a newspaper while the woman toyed with her hair before the mirror on the dresser.

"Excuse me!" Joe said. "We must be in the wrong room!"

"No, we're not," said Frank. "This is ours—Number Seven."

The woman turned and smiled. "Oh, you must be the Hardy brothers," she said. "The manager moved your luggage out."

"What for?" Frank asked, puzzled and annoyed. "We're registered here overnight."

Then he realized there was no use in arguing. It apparently was not the couple's fault. Frank and Joe hastened to the manager's office. The man smiled broadly. "Well, I've done as you asked. You have a very nice little bungalow and I know you'll enjoy it."

"Wh-what?" asked Joe.

"Your college friends relayed your message," the man said, stroking his bald head.

The Hardys were dumbfounded but listened to the

manager's explanation. "Three boys came here and told me you Hardys wanted one of the cottages where it would be quieter. So we moved you in there bag and baggage." The man added, "It costs only two dollars more a night. You're getting a bargain."

"Where is this cottage?" Joe asked.

"Over there," the man said, pointing to one of the little houses. It was lighted inside.

The boys hastened over, and as they passed the window they saw a stocky youth standing inside. Frank flung open the door. "What's the meaning of this?" he demanded.

The young man whirled round. Frank and Joe saw that he was wearing a black half-mask. At the same time, the cupboard door burst open and out jumped four other masked youths.

"Hey, what kind of a joke is this!" Joe cried out as the intruders jumped both Hardys. They struggled furiously, but the combined weight of the masked boys finally bore Frank and Joe to the floor. They were bound and gagged, then tied securely to two long planks.

Without saying a word, the Hardys' assailants loaded them into an estate car parked behind the cottage. They were driven out of the motel grounds and along the main highway for several miles. Then the driver turned left on to a side road and stopped a mile farther on.

The brothers were lifted out, carried a short distance through some low brush, and laid crosswise on a railway track. Then the masked quintet vanished into the darkness.

Frank squirmed and tugged at his bonds. Joe did too,

but neither boy could loosen the ropes which secured them. Beads of perspiration stood out on their foreheads. Then came a sound which struck terror into their hearts. In the distance they heard the ominous growl of an approaching diesel engine!

·4·

Tricked!

CASTING hopeless glances at each other, Frank and Joe struggled desperately at their bonds while the diesel engine drew closer.

The rumble of the wheels grew deafening. But then, as if by a miracle, the engine throbbed past, leaving only the clickety-clack of freight cars trailing in its wake.

Unscathed but shaken, Frank and Joe continued to work at the ropes which secured them to the planks. By straining until his muscles ached, Frank stretched his bound wrists to where he could dimly see a spike protruding from a railway sleeper. Over and over he snagged the knot upon the spike. Each effort loosened the rope a little more. Finally it fell open.

With his wrists released, Frank tore out his gag and reached over to do the same for Joe.

"Whew!" Joe gasped. "I thought our goose was cooked!"

"It would have been an awful way to say goodbye to mother earth," Frank replied grimly, quickly freeing himself from the plank.

Then he released his brother. The two boys stood up and stretched painfully, massaging their cramped muscles. Twenty yards away the polished rails of another railway line glimmered in the moonlight.

"Look, these tracks we were on are rusty," Frank noted.

"Must be a siding," Joe said, "which isn't used any more."

"A great way to give a guy grey hair at a tender age," Frank remarked.

"It wasn't funny," Joe said, between clenched teeth.

"I'll say not," his brother agreed. "I'd like to find the nut who planned this trick!"

"If I see him first, I'll take care of that joker," Joe said.

After walking along the tracks some distance, the boys came to the highway. There they flagged a friendly truck driver, who readily agreed to drive them to their motel.

Jouncing up and down in the cab beside the driver, the Hardys continued to speculate.

"You suppose what happened to us was just a crazy mix-up?" Joe asked in low tones. "Why should those fellows pick on us?"

Frank frowned. "I have a hunch the whole thing was intended to scare us away from Kenworthy before we could find a good clue."

"Then you think Todd could have been kidnapped?"

"Let's not rule out that possibility," Frank said.

As the truck approached the Palm Court grounds, Joe suddenly chuckled. "If Chet and Biff wanted excitement—they should've been with us tonight. Honeycomb Caves must be pretty tame compared with the Kenworthy capers."

Frank grinned widely. "Chet would've lost ten pounds from fright."

The truck swung over and stopped. The Hardys hopped out, thanking the driver for the lift.

"Sure thing, fellows. So long."

The brothers made a beeline for the office.

"Now to question Baldy," Frank said. He stabbed the buzzer beside the door repeatedly until a light shone inside. The manager, sleepy-eyed and holding up his trousers with one hand, opened the door. He was not in a good mood.

"What do you mean by waking me up at this hour?" he asked crossly. "If you're going to check out, wait till morning, for Pete's sake."

"Somebody else checked us out," Frank said. "We'd like to ask you some questions."

Alarmed by the boys' determination, the manager let them in. There the Hardys learned that the instigator of the room switch was a member of a local fraternity at Kenworthy College.

"I thought these college kids were just going to have some fun with you," the man said.

"The police might give it a different label," Frank replied grimly. "Now, what's this fellow's name and where does he live?"

After the man had jotted down the information, Frank and Joe drove directly to the Delta Sigma fraternity house. Dawn lay like a pink halo on the eastern horizon, but the Hardys' thoughts were anything but heavenly as they rapped on the fraternity house door. No one answered. Joe rang the bell while Frank continued banging.

Finally a young fellow in pyjamas opened up and yawned in Frank's face. "Whatever it is, we don't want any," he said, then started to close the door.

Frank reached for his shoulder and whirled him about. "This isn't any joke," he said. "We're looking for Jack Hale."

"Oh, the president," the youth said, stifling another yawn. "I can't wake him up—he's special."

"I'll say he is," Joe declared.

"But you fellows don't understand." The college boy regarded the Hardys earnestly with his pale blue eyes. "We don't wake the fraternity president until eight o'clock. He doesn't have his first class until nine."

"He's going to have a lesson right now," Frank said sternly. "Get him up!"

The youth shrugged, and padded off in bare feet to the second floor. Listening below, the boys heard shouts and angry words, preceding the appearance of a thick-set youth several years older than the Hardys. In red and white striped pyjamas he thumped down the stairs. When he saw Frank and Joe, he stopped with a startled expression.

"Isn't it kind of early—" Jack Hale started to say.

"Not for a punch in the jaw," Joe declared hotly, and stepped forward with fists cocked.

"Wait a minute, Joe," Frank said. "Let's get some questions answered before you start swinging." He walked over to Hale, who backed away nervously. "I'll put it on the line," Frank said. "What's the idea of leaving us on the railway track? And why did you switch our motel room?"

"Wait a minute, fellows! Hold it!" Hale said. "We

thought you'd guess it was just a little testing job. Anyway, why are you getting so worked up?"

"Yes, why?" the blue-eyed youth put in.

Hale continued, "You two were never in any *real* danger. We had a lookout posted to keep an eye on you in case you needed help. Say, you are going to be Delta Sigma students, aren't you?"

"Of course not," said Joe, his biceps still flexed.

"So you were having us on?" asked Frank. "Who told you to do that?"

Jack Hale looked embarrassed. He cast a fleeting glance up the stairs and seemed relieved when several other Delta Sigma boys moved quietly down behind him.

"I can't tell you who it is," Hale said.

The blue-eyed youth nodded vigorously. "We're honour bound not to reveal his identity."

"We thought you were going to be Delta Sigma men," Jack said. "Honest we did."

"Well, then, you ought to let prospective students in on it too," Frank said. He turned away. "Come on, Joe. Let's get out of here. We have work to do."

Looking somewhat the worse for wear after their strenuous night, the Hardys nonetheless planned another bit of sleuthing before returning to their cottage for sleep.

"Let's examine Todd's room before Quill gets up," Frank suggested.

Joe readily agreed. "At six a.m. Quill's probably still asleep." Joe reached into his pocket. "I have the key to Todd's apartment."

The Hardys encountered a few milk delivery trucks

and one newspaper boy as they made their way to
Shelly Row. Joe inserted the key quietly and turned it
in the lock. The boys entered. Frank pressed his ear
against the apartment wall. Silence.

"He's still in the arms of Morpheus," Frank whispered.

"Okay," Joe said. "Let's look around."

Enough daylight filtered through the two front
windows to allow the boys to examine the apartment
carefully. While Joe concentrated on objects of furni-
ture, Frank looked through notes and textbooks lying
about. But the boys could find no evidence as to where
Morgan Todd might have gone.

"I guess the police search was pretty thorough, after
all," Joe commented. "What are you looking at,
Frank?"

His brother held one of the mimeographed examination sheets in his hand and was scrutinizing it. Joe
watched Frank as he scanned sentence after sentence
on the white paper. Then a strange expression came over
his face. Joe had seen it before when Frank was on the
trail of a clue.

"You found something?" Joe asked excitedly.

"I'll say I have!" Frank declared, sucking in his
breath. "Wow! Look at this!"

· 5 ·

Counter-attack

JOE glanced over his brother's shoulder. "All I see is an exam paper—the fill-in type."

"Yes," Frank replied. "But there's a clue right under your nose."

"I don't get it, Frank. You must have super vision."

"Look. Read the first question, Joe."

" 'Russia's present political system was founded by ——' "

"I don't care about the answer," Frank said. "Now read the second question."

" 'Only —— men from California have been named to the Supreme Court.' "

Joe frowned. "It's still a riddle to me."

Enjoying the game he was playing, Frank asked, "How many questions are there?"

"Eight."

"And the first letter of the first word in each question spells what?"

Joe's eyes quickly roved down the side of the exam sheet. "R-O-C-K-A-W-A-Y." He whistled. "The name of a town!"

"That's it—Rockaway," Frank said. "Todd did leave a clue. And I don't think the police found it, either."

"Good for you," Joe said, slapping his brother on the back. "I guess I'm too exhausted for any deep brainwork."

"We'll have breakfast before we turn in," Frank said. "Then we'll go to the post office and find out from their guidebook how many Rockaways there are in the U.S."

"There's probably at least twenty-five," Joe said with a sigh. "By the time we check on them, Morgan Todd could be in Timbuktu." He yawned deeply, then placed his ear to the apartment wall.

"Hear anything?" asked Frank.

"Bouncy Quill is up," Joe said. "Let's get out of here before he discovers us. He'd be sure to ask a lot of questions."

Because the campus cafeteria was not yet open, Frank and Joe stopped at an all-night café on the outskirts of town. After eating a hearty breakfast, they returned to their cottage.

"Oh boy, now for a peaceful sleep," Joe said. He kicked off his shoes and flung himself on top of the bedspread.

Too exhausted to undress, Frank did the same. The boys slept soundly for several hours.

Frank awakened first and thought he was having a nightmare. A pillow was pressed hard over his face and a powerful hand pinned his shoulder to the mattress.

Trying to cry out, Frank kicked wildly and flung the intruder away from the bed. Someone hit the opposite wall with a thud and crashed to the floor. The noise aroused Joe, who sprang up, wild-eyed, and looked around the room.

"Jumpin' catfish!" Joe glared at the stunned figure

on the floor. "Biff Hooper, what're you doing here?"

Biff aroused himself and shook his head. "Got to clear the cobwebs," he said. "I was only fooling, Frank. You jumped me like a wounded panther."

Frank laughed. "You got off easy, boy."

At that moment Chet sauntered through the doorway, munching noisily on potato crisps. He dipped into a huge cellophane bag and pressed another handful into his mouth. Still munching, he asked, "What's all the racket?"

"Biff making a grand entrance," Frank said wryly. "Sit down, fellows. We'll tell you our latest news. How about some crisps, Chet?"

The stout lad proffered the crinkly bag, and the Hardys helped themselves. As they ate, they briefed Biff and Chet on their findings at Kenworthy College and their harrowing experience of the previous night.

"Wowie!" Biff exclaimed. "You Hardys sure stir things up!"

"And now," Joe said, "we have to find out how many Rockaways there are in the U.S.A."

"I can tell you one," Chet said. "It's near Honeycomb Caves."

"I never heard of it," Frank said in surprise.

"Neither did I," said Chet. "It's a dinky place."

Biff explained that they had driven down the coast early that morning and stopped at a small petrol station a couple of miles north of Rockaway. "We asked the attendant how to get to Honeycomb Caves," he went on, "and he warned us not to go."

"Why?" Frank asked.

"He said awful things might happen to us if we did."

"Something very strange is going on there," added Chet with a great air of knowledge. "It sounded like a real mystery so we thought maybe you'd like to take time out and look into it."

"I knew you'd try to snag us into going to those caves," said Frank, chuckling.

Chet flung out his arms dramatically. "After all, Biff and I thought sure you would've found Morgan Todd by this time!"

"It's not going to be so easy," Frank said. With a wink at his brother, he added, "But thanks for thinking about us. Come on, Joe! Our first stop's the post office." He glanced down at his dishevelled clothes and grinned. "I mean, after the shower."

Fifteen minutes later both boys were in fresh clothes and Joe said, "Okay, let's go."

He was about to step out of the door when he suddenly closed it and motioned to the others. "I think we're in for a fight, fellows, so get ready."

"What's the matter?" Frank asked, and looked out of the window.

Across the broad lawns of the Palm Court Motel strode four youths. In the lead was Jack Hale!

"Delta Sigmas," Joe said tersely. "Maybe the ones who made trouble for us last night. If they think it's four against two, they're mistaken."

"Right!" said Biff, who liked nothing more than playing tackle on the Bayport High football team.

"Okay," said Frank. "You and Chet hide in the cupboard." Then, opening the door, he politely invited the four fraternity men to enter.

"Hi," Jack said with a half-smile. "We have a little surprise for you."

But before he could utter another word, the cupboard door was flung open. Biff bolted across the room, taking a flying leap at two of the college boys. Chet pounced on the third. Only Jack remained standing. His face bore a pained expression.

"We don't want to fight!" he said.

"Then what did you barge in on us for?" Joe demanded.

Biff dragged two of the students to their feet, and Frank said, "Okay, let's smoke the peace pipe. What's up, Jack?"

Embarrassed, the fraternity president said that he had come to offer Frank and Joe invitations to join Delta Sigma should they decide to attend Kenworthy College.

"You're the kind we like," he said. "Plenty of guts!"

"Thanks for the invite," Joe said coolly. "We'll keep it in mind if you tell us who put you up to that low-down trick last night."

Jack looked at the floor and the Hardys could see that he was torn between loyalty to the unknown perpetrator and regard for them.

"Really, I can't tell," he said finally. "You wouldn't want me to rat on a pal."

"No hard feelings," said Frank, though he thought the youth was foolish to protect such a person. Then he introduced Biff and Chet.

"Wow!" said one of the college boys. "We could use you two on the Kenworthy football team."

With that, the Delta Sigmas left.

Frank drove the Bayporters to the post office, located beside the town hall. A helpful clerk passed the postal directory over the counter and Frank thumbed through its pages.

"Hey, look at this," he said. "There are only three Rockaways—one in Oregon, one in New Jersey, and the other on the coast down from Bayport."

"It's certain we won't go to Oregon or New Jersey first," Chet said. "You fellows will investigate the closest one or I miss my bet."

"O genius of a treasure hunter!" declaimed Joe, as he placed the right palm of his hand on his forehead and bowed low. "We, your humble servants, salaam!"

The others guffawed at the sudden look of embarrassment that swept over Chet's face as he cast his eyes quickly round the post office to see if anybody was watching. Seeing no one, Chet joined in the laughter.

Frank handed back the directory to the grinning clerk and thanked him. The boys, still laughing, trooped out of the post office.

"Well, our next destination—Rockaway!" Frank said. He added thoughtfully, "You know, this isn't a bad move. We'll leave here as if we've been stymied on our investigation."

"That's right," Joe said. "So if anyone has been tracking us, they'll think we've given up." As an afterthought he added, "We ought to thank Cadmus Quill and the dean before we leave."

"Let me go too. Maybe I won't see the inside of a college again," Chet quipped.

The four drove to the campus, parked, and entered the administration building.

Dean Eastland, as before, was courteous to his callers. After thanking Frank and Joe for their interest in the case, he promised to relay any new information to them.

"By the way, Dean Eastland," Frank said, "would you send us the roster of Delta Sigma fraternity?"

"Of course," the dean replied, and jotted down their Bayport address.

As the boys walked into the hallway they met Cadmus Quill.

"We're going back to Bayport," Frank told him. "I'm sorry we couldn't find your friend Todd."

"Anyhow," said Joe, "thanks for your help, Mr Quill."

"Not at all," replied the instructor as he shook hands with the two boys. "I'm sure there's no need to worry. I feel strongly that he's in Europe—probably already married."

"It's possible," Frank said. "Well, perhaps we'll see you again."

"Come on, fellows," Biff said as they left the building. "If I hang around this college campus any longer I'll be as smart as you are."

"I'm itching for Honeycomb Caves," Chet bantered. "I feel in the need for some ready doubloons."

As the boys hastened back to the Hardy car, Frank had the feeling that Cadmus Quill had followed them out of the building. When he slid behind the wheel he glanced into his rear-view mirror.

There stood Quill on the steps, gazing at them intently. Then he turned back to the door.

Suddenly, above the sound of the starter motor,

Chet let out an Indian war whoop and yelled, "On to Rockaway!"

Frank, with his eyes still on the rear-view mirror, saw Quill stiffen and spin around.

·6·

The Toppled Tower

CADMUS QUILL stood on the steps and stared at the boys with a startled look on his round face.

"That remark hit home!" Frank thought. He got out of the car and ran up to Quill before he had a chance to retreat. "You seem interested in Rockaway," Frank said bluntly, hoping to catch him off guard. "Do you know somebody there?"

Quill smiled. "I thought for a moment," he replied casually, "that your friend had said *Far* Rockaway, in New York. I have an uncle who lives there."

Frank was momentarily at a loss about how to pursue his line of questioning. This gave Quill time to turn on his heel. He strode off, saying, "I have a lecture to prepare. Good luck to you!"

Frank returned to the car, and as the boys drove back to the motel he discussed with them Quill's peculiar actions.

Joe spoke up. "That uncle bit doesn't ring true. Quill is keeping back something, I'll bet."

"Why should the name Rockaway strike him?" Chet wondered.

"Who knows?" Joe said. "Maybe he discovered the Rockaway clue in Todd's exam."

"I don't get it," Frank said, as he parked in front of the cottage. "Quill knows we're detectives. If he did find the Rockaway clue, why didn't he tell us?"

"Maybe he wants to follow it himself," Joe replied.

"This Cadmus Quill will bear watching," remarked Biff, now thoroughly caught up in the excitement of the mystery.

Chet suggested that while the Hardys were packing, he and Biff would take his jalopy to a service station. "We want to check it out before starting the trip to Rockaway," Chet said.

The brothers entered their quarters. While Joe tossed his belongings into his suitcase, Frank telephoned Bayport. Mr Hardy answered.

"Frank," he said, "I'm glad you called!" The boy was surprised at his father's clipped tone.

"What's the matter, Dad?" he asked.

"I'm afraid you and Joe will have to come home right away. It's urgent, and I'd rather not take time to explain it."

"Okay, Dad. But just one thing," Frank added quickly. "We're suspicious of a fellow named Cadmus Quill. Will you get us a confidential report on him, please?" Mr Hardy promised and Frank hung up. "Something's gone haywire in Bayport," he said to his brother, then repeated their father's message.

While Frank packed his belongings, Joe hustled over to the motel office to pay their bill. He returned to the car just as Frank was stowing the luggage into the boot. At the same moment, Biff and Chet drove up.

"All set for the big adventure at Honeycomb Caves!" Chet sang out exuberantly. "Joe, Frank, I bet I get better mileage than you boys on the way to the coast."

When the Hardys did not smile at the boast, Biff sensed something was wrong. "What's the matter, fellows?"

"We can't go with you—at least not now," said Frank.

"Sorry to leave you in the lurch like this," Joe added, as he slid behind the wheel.

Frank told them about their father's cryptic message.

"Well, if you're needed in Bayport, I guess that's that," Chet commented.

"We'll join you as soon as we can," Frank promised.

"We'll be camping on the beach," Chet said.

Grinning, Joe started the car. "So long, and don't join any fraternities!"

Joe held the speedometer needle at the maximum speed allowed, and the countryside flashed by. When they hit the turnpike, Frank took turns with his brother at the wheel. Now, with greater speed, the miles melted past.

"She purrs like a kitten," Frank said. "A great car, Joe."

"Good thing we had the engine tuned," Frank remarked as the wind whipped through his hair.

After a quick stop for lunch, Joe drove away from the roadside restaurant.

"Want to listen to the news?"

"Okay. What country's having a war today?"

"Maybe someone has landed on Jupiter," Frank said as he clicked on the high-powered transistor.

The first word to hit their ears was "Bayport." Joe took his foot off the accelerator and Frank turned up the volume. The newscaster's report sent a shiver up their spines: *The radar tower on Telescope Hill had toppled over in a high wind!*

"This must be the emergency Dad meant," Frank said. "Come on. Let's go."

Joe guided the car expertly along the motorway, and, slightly under six hours since they had left the town of Kenworthy, the Hardys pulled into their driveway.

As the boys carried their luggage in at the back door, Mrs Hardy met them.

"Hi, Mother," said Frank. "Where's Dad?"

"At the radar site. He didn't have time to tell you all about it on the phone."

"We heard the report on the car radio," said Joe.

"Your father wants you to go right over," Mrs Hardy said.

The boys carried the suitcases to their rooms, splashed cold water on their faces and hurried back to the car.

As they neared the construction site, traffic was slowed by the large trucks plying back and forth to the installation.

Finally they reached the gate. Frank parked the car, and he and Joe approached the guard. The brothers identified themselves.

"Our father is waiting for us inside," Frank said.

With a nod of recognition the security man admitted them. Briskly Frank and Joe trotted up the incline which led to the top of Telescope Hill.

Joe gave a low whistle as they neared the toppled tower. It had cut a jagged scar in the woodland and lay twisted and broken. A number of men were inspecting it. Mr Hardy, with a magnifying glass in one hand, was examining a girder at a point about five feet from the ground, where the steel superstructure had snapped off.

"You made good time," the detective said as his sons ran up. He added quickly, "I'm sorry, but I won't need you after all, boys. I found what I was looking for, soon after I summoned you."

"What's that, Dad?" asked Frank.

"Look here," the detective said, and handed him the magnifying glass.

The young sleuth studied the break in the steel. "I'll say you found something! Here, take a look, Joe."

The younger boy also was amazed as he noticed that the break was smooth and clean except for a burr at the edge of the girder.

"This was cut almost all the way through to weaken the structure," said Joe, "but I don't see any saw marks."

"It was probably done with an electronic cutter," Mr Hardy remarked. "I've already reported this to the government men. Their chief engineer agrees with my theory."

"And the high wind finished the job?" asked Joe.

"Exactly," his father replied. He added that the saboteur had cut the line so straight and deep that the girder had been snapped off like a crisp cracker.

"We're up against a daring and well-equipped ring of saboteurs," Frank commented, as the three walked alongside the fallen tower.

"But I wasn't sure of that at first," Mr Hardy said. "That's why I needed you. I wanted you to do some undercover work to help me find out whether it really was sabotage." He added that he had not revealed the nature of his urgent request for fear someone might have tapped his phone line. "I didn't want anyone to find out what I suspected."

"Any information on Cadmus Quill?" Joe asked, as they passed beneath a tall pine tree, the top of which had been sheared off by the tower.

"Nothing yet," Mr Hardy said. "A very reliable agency is checking into it. They'll send me the report in code."

Suddenly the detective yelled, "Look out!" and gave Joe a push which sent him sprawling headlong on to the grass. Simultaneously a huge chunk of metal thudded to the ground inches from his body.

"Good grief! Where'd that come from?" Frank cried, looking up into the tall pine.

"A piece of the tower must have broken off and got stuck in the branches," Mr Hardy said. "You all right, Joe?"

The boy picked himself up, took a deep breath, and grinned. "Being a detective can be dangerous!" he said. "Thanks for the assistance."

The three Hardys went through the main gate. "Our car is parked close to yours, Dad," Frank said.

A short time later father and sons entered their house together. After a late dinner with Mrs Hardy, the tired sleuths turned in.

When the boys came down for breakfast the next morning they found their father already up.

"There's a letter for you, boys," he said, pointing to the hall table.

Frank picked up the long heavy envelope. "It's from

Dean Eastland," he said. "Must be the fraternity roster."

As he spoke, the doorbell rang and Joe hurried to answer. It was a telegram for Mr Hardy.

"The report on Quill," Joe said eagerly.

"Bring it into my office," his father said, leading the way.

The detective opened the telegram and studied the mysteriously coded message. Taking a pencil and pad, he unscrambled the code letter by letter. His sons looked on intently over his shoulder. The information was concise. "Cadmus Quill. Good student. Good family. Good reputation. Likes to travel. Made an extended tour of study abroad three years ago."

"But look at the country he studied in!" Frank said excitedly.

Joe whistled. "The same one Todd visited last summer!"

"Dad," Frank exclaimed, "do you know what this could mean?"

.7.

The Palais Paris

"I GET it!" Joe burst out. "Both Quill and Todd were brainwashed into helping a foreign power!"

Mr Hardy spoke up. "Frank, what's your opinion?"

"My theory," Frank said, "is that maybe Todd and Quill had opposing views about this unfriendly country. Joe's jumping to conclusions and maybe I am too, but—"

Frank dropped into a thoughtful silence.

"Go on," Mr Hardy encouraged him. "You may be on the right track."

"If Todd was against the country and Quill for it, maybe they had a quarrel."

"Which could have led to Todd's disappearance?" Joe asked.

His brother nodded. "And whoever ordered the fraternity to trick us in order to scare us off," he added, "is in on the plot." Frank was still holding the letter from Dean Eastland. "Maybe this will give us a clue." He slit open the envelope and withdrew a printed pamphlet.

Frank's eyebrows shot up. "Oh—oh!" he exclaimed. "Here's our answer!" He slapped the booklet down on his father's desk and pointed to the words on the cover:

54

Delta Sigma Fraternity—Cadmus Quill, Faculty Adviser. "He probably was behind the trickery."

Mr Hardy glanced at Frank and said, "That certainly fits in with your theory."

"Yes," Joe agreed. "I think the police ought to question Quill."

Mr Hardy also thought this would be a good idea, so Frank telephoned the police chief at Kenworthy. He told the officer what he had just learned. The chief thanked him and promised to call the Hardys back after he had interrogated Quill.

Later, just as the family was sitting down to breakfast, the phone rang. Frank answered. "Oh, hello, Chief," he said. "Any luck with Quill?"

Mr Hardy and Joe jumped up from the table when they heard Frank exclaim in astonishment:

"He did? . . . All right. Thanks a lot . . . You'll keep us posted? . . . Right . . . Goodbye."

"What's the scoop?" Joe asked eagerly.

"More mystery," Frank said. "Now Quill has disappeared!"

Joe gave a low whistle. "Kidnapped?"

"Maybe."

Mr Hardy's brow furrowed. "You boys could be close to the truth about that foreign country's being involved," he said. "Maybe both Todd and Quill were whisked away because of some political information they gleaned."

Frank went on to report that the Kenworthy police had issued a seven-state missing person alarm for Cadmus Quill. "Only when he's found," Frank added, "can we tell whether Quill is friend or foe."

Various aspects of the case were discussed by the detective and his sons during the meal. What move to make next was the question. Mr Hardy said that since sabotage was definitely indicated at the radar site, he could free his sons to concentrate on the Todd matter.

"I vote we look for Quill," Joe suggested, as Mrs Hardy sliced a broad wedge of home-made coffee cake for Frank.

"Umm! Great as usual, Mom," Frank remarked, having disposed of a generous bite. "What do you say, Dad? Shall we follow up the Rockaway clue?"

"Maybe Joe has a point," Mr Hardy replied. "I have a definite feeling that if you find Quill you'll find Todd."

Joe grinned at his brother. "Lucky our bags are still packed."

The boys had gone to their room to bring down the luggage when the phone rang. Fenton Hardy was first to pick up the receiver in his study.

The caller was Chet Morton who said that he wanted all three Hardys to hear his story.

"Hold on. I'll get Frank and Joe on the other wires."

In a few moments Frank was at the hall phone, and Joe at the upstairs extension. "Are you all there now?" Chet's voice was edged with excitement.

"Right," Joe said. "What's up?"

"Maybe *you* can tell *me*," Chet said. "What is this guy Quill anyhow? A maniac?"

"Quill?" Frank echoed as his father and brother gasped in amazement. "Have you seen him?"

"Seen him! I'll say so," Chet replied. "I think he's out of his head."

"Come on, boy! Give us the lowdown!" Joe prompted.

"Quill forced our car off the road on the way to Rockaway, that's what!" Chet said.

"Did he follow you all the way from the college?" Fenton Hardy put in.

Chet said that must have been the case. "After a while Biff noticed somebody trailing us."

"How did you know it was Quill?" asked Frank.

Chet told of stopping for a traffic light. The other car had lingered several lengths behind. "But we recognized his moonface!" Chet said triumphantly.

Several miles farther on, as he and Biff rounded a curve, Quill's car had cut them off.

"My old jalopy scraped against a tree," Chet went on. "Biff got a bump on the head, but otherwise we weren't injured. It ruined the paintwork, though."

"I'm sure glad it wasn't any worse," Frank said.

"Did Quill keep on going?" Joe asked.

"Yes. In the direction of Rockaway. Say, why don't you fellows come down here and protect Biff and me?"

"Not a bad idea," said Frank. "Where shall we meet you?"

"We'll go on to Rockaway and set up our tent on the beach," Chet replied.

"Okay," Joe put in. "Get there as soon we can."

After Mr Hardy added his approval to the plan, the Hardys said goodbye and hung up.

The three detectives were perplexed about Biff and Chet's brush with Cadmus Quill. "Why would he pick on them?" Joe mused.

Frank shook his head. "My hunch is Quill thought you and I were in that car, Joe!"

Mr Hardy added a word of caution. "Don't take unnecessary risks, boys. Your enemies are dangerous."

As the brothers were about to leave, their mother said, "Oh, by the way, I have an errand I'd like you to do."

"Anything for you, Mother," said Frank, kissing her on the cheek.

"Well, it's really for Aunt Gertrude."

Joe rolled his eyes. "Oh—oh. Is Aunty coming for another visit?"

When Mrs Hardy nodded, Joe remarked, "It's just as well we're leaving for Rockaway now. Aunt Gertrude wouldn't approve of this mystery, I'll bet!"

Miss Gertrude Hardy was actually a great favourite with the boys despite her tart tongue and frequent predictions of dire mishaps overtaking her sleuthing nephews.

Frank chuckled. "What's the big deal for Aunt Gertrude?"

"Get her a spinning wheel."

"But—" Joe gulped. "Where're we ever going to find one?"

"Perhaps at the Palais Paris," Mrs Hardy replied with a twinkle.

"Wow!" Joe exclaimed. "Sounds real fancy—what is it?"

Mrs Hardy explained that there was a new and very attractive French restaurant on the main highway near Rockaway. "I understand," she added, "that the restaurant has an antique shop connected with it. It's only a few miles from where you're going. I checked it on the road map."

The boys grimaced slightly at the idea of having to bargain for an old spinning-wheel, but assured their mother they would pick one up if available.

"Wonderful," said Mrs Hardy. "I think your aunt will be here by the time you return."

Frank and Joe hurriedly stowed their luggage in the car. Their parents came to say goodbye. "Watch out for those saboteurs at the radar site, Dad," Frank said.

"I intend to. Good luck yourselves."

Both boys hugged their mother, shook hands with their father and hopped into the car.

"The camping equipment is already in the boot," Joe said. "Have we forgotten anything, Frank?"

"We're all set," his brother replied, giving the circle sign with his thumb and forefinger.

The morning was grey and foggy as the boys set off with Joe at the wheel, but an hour later the sun shone through and burned off the mist.

The coastline now assumed roller-coaster proportions as they approached the Honeycomb Caves area. The highway was about two hundred feet above sea-level. A short plateau extended to the lip of the palisades to the left of them before dropping down abruptly into the Atlantic Ocean.

"The caves are below these cliffs somewhere," declared Joe, motioning towards the coastal side. The sea, hidden most of the time by a thick stand of woods and undergrowth, occasionally flashed through in brilliant glimmers.

Presently they approached a rambling, attractive

building with stone trim and a wide porch. "There's the Palais Paris," said Frank, pointing to a sign on a lamp-post announcing the fashionable restaurant. It was set thirty feet back from the right side of the road with a neat parking area beside it. The lanes, marked with white paint, were nearly filled with expensive new cars.

"A good crowd for lunch," Joe remarked, as he pulled in and parked.

The brothers got out and walked towards the entrance to the antique shop located next to the restaurant in the same building. As they passed the open door, Frank noted the well-dressed patrons seated at the tables. There was also a sign tacked to a post beside the door. It read: WAITRESSES WANTED.

"A ritzy place, I'd say, Joe," he remarked. "And if they have a big selection of antiques we ought to be able to find Aunt Gertrude her spinning-wheel."

The boys entered the shop and looked round. The broad floorboards were pegged, giving the place an old-fashioned appearance. Several long tables were filled with ancient-looking articles such as candle moulds, clocks, pewter pieces and bed-warmers. From the low ceiling hung a black iron pot and several oil lamps.

"Hey, over there, Frank!" Joe pointed to one corner of the room, where a spinning-wheel was suspended on two hooks fastened to the ceiling.

"Just what we're looking for." Frank walked over to inspect the wheel. Joe followed.

"Why have they got it hanging in mid-air?" he wondered.

"For the effect, I guess," Frank replied. He looked about for a sales assistant. Meantime, Joe tried to lift the wheel from its supporting hooks.

A resounding *crack* made Frank whirl about, just in time to see the spinning-wheel fall to pieces over Joe's head. They landed on the floor with a clatter.

"Leapin' frogs!" Frank exclaimed. "How'd that happen?"

"I don't know," Joe said. "I only touched it."

The noise brought a woman running from the back of the shop. She was tall, with dark eyes and black hair which was pulled back into a knot. "Oh, what have you done!" she cried with a pronounced French accent, putting her hands to her head.

"Nothing!" Joe protested. "The old wheel just came apart like matchsticks."

"We wanted to buy it," Frank said. "It must not have been very well made."

"That piece was valuable," the woman declared indignantly. "It was not for sale." She wrung her hands. "It was for show only—to set off our beautiful antique display."

Joe was embarrassed. "I'm sorry," he said. "Maybe we can put it back together again." He picked up the large wheel and the spindle, still intact.

"*Non!*" The woman's eyes flashed. "You do not get away so easily. I am the manageress here. You will have to pay for this wheel."

Joe groaned. "Why didn't I keep my hands off it!"

"You will pay!" the woman repeated. She hastened into the back of the shop and returned seconds later with a tall, burly, well-muscled man.

"Marcel," she said, "you will know how to handle this."

"These the kids?" he growled.

"Yes," the woman replied. "They refuse to make good for this spinning-wheel which they have so carelessly broken."

Joe opened his mouth to object, but Frank nudged him to silence. The muscular man advanced on them threateningly. In a low voice he rumbled, "I advise you to give us the money and be on your way!"

·8·

The Old Man's Warning

FRANK, although angry, wished to avoid a fight. He and Joe were on a sleuthing mission—this must come first. "How much do we owe you?" Frank asked the belligerent man. At the answer, Frank shook his head. "We don't have enough money, but I'll leave my watch for security."

Marcel sniffed. "Let's see it."

Frank slipped off the handsome stainless-steel time-piece which he had received the Christmas before. "It's a good Swiss make," he said.

As Marcel examined the watch, Joe took twenty dollars from his pocket. "How about twenty dollars and the watch?" he asked. "That should be enough for a broken old spinning-wheel."

Marcel glanced at the woman and she gave a barely perceptible nod.

"Okay," he said. "But don't come around here again breakin' up our antiques."

"We'll be back," Frank said, "with the thirty dollars to redeem my watch."

The shop manageress grudgingly produced a card-board carton into which Frank and Joe placed the spinning-wheel parts. Then they put the box in the boot of their car.

As Frank drove off, he said, "Something phoney going on here. That spinning-wheel was only slapped together."

"Looks like the whole shop might have been set up in an awful hurry," Joe remarked. "I'll bet most of the other stuff is junk too."

"I wonder how Aunt Gertrude's going to like her antique," Frank said, with an ear-to-ear grin.

"I hate to think!" Joe said wryly, taking a road map from the glove compartment.

After studying it for a moment, he announced, "We're not far from Rockaway now. Boy! It's really a small speck on the map!"

Frank laughed. "I hope we don't miss the place."

Presently he drove down a long hill, and the Hardys found themselves in Rockaway. It was nothing more than a small crossroads village on the shore adjacent to a fishing pier. The brothers soon came to the camping site on the beach and parked. They spotted Biff and Chet sunning themselves before their tent. As the Hardys parked on the shoulder of the road, their friends hurried over.

Frank and Joe got out and looked at Chet's damaged jalopy.

"Wow! That's a bad dent!" Joe said. "Cadmus Quill didn't pull any punches."

"You can say that again!" Biff retorted.

"I think he's got it in for all of us!"

"Have you looked for him around here?" Frank asked.

"Look for yourself," Chet replied with a sweep of his hand. "There's nothing but a couple of stores and a few shacks."

True, Rockaway could hardly be called a town. It was a sleepy little place, quite picturesque and redolent of fish. A weather-beaten building stood across the street. Above the door was a large sign: TUTTLE'S GENERAL STORE.

"Let's stock up on grub," Frank said. He and Joe took rucksacks from their car and the four boys headed for the store.

A venerable man with whiskers was seated behind a counter. He was intently scrutinizing a newspaper.

The old gentleman put aside the newspaper and regarded them through his thick-lensed spectacles with grave curiosity, as though they were some new specimen of humanity.

"You're Mr Tuttle?" Frank ventured.

"Yup. What can I do for you?"

"We'd like to know how far it is to Honeycomb Caves."

The man's eyes widened. "Honeycomb Caves!" he repeated in a high, cracked voice. "You lads going to pass by there?"

Chet spoke up. "No, we're going to camp in the caves and do some beachcombing." He told of his metal detector and how they hoped to locate some washed-up treasure.

Mr Tuttle leaned over the counter. "You— you're goin' to camp in Honeycomb Caves!" he exclaimed incredulously.

"Why, yes," Joe said.

The storekeeper shook his head solemnly. "You're new in these parts, aren't you?"

"From Bayport," Frank offered. "This is the first time we've been down this way."

"I thought so," returned the bewhiskered man with a great air of satisfaction, as though his judgment had been verified.

"Tell us," Frank said patiently, "how much farther do we have to go to reach Honeycomb Caves?"

"It's a matter of five miles by the road. Then you'll have to walk a bit."

"Is there a place we can pitch our tent?" Chet asked.

"Oh, yes. A fisherman lives nearby—name of John Donachie. He might allow you to camp near his cottage. But if I was you, I wouldn't do no campin' thereabouts. That is," Mr Tuttle added, "unless you stay away from the caves."

"We'd like to explore them," Joe said.

The old fellow gasped. "Explore 'em! Lads, you're crazy!"

"Is it against the law?" Chet inquired.

"No, it ain't. But it's against common sense."

"Why?" asked Biff.

"It just is," the storekeeper retorted, as though that explained everything.

"You mean the caves are dangerous?" queried Frank, enjoying the conversation.

"Maybe, maybe," returned their informant mysteriously. "If you take my advice, you'll stay away from 'em."

Joe rested his elbows on the counter. "Can't you at least tell us the reason?"

Mr Tuttle seemed to relish the boys' attention. "Well," he went on, "some mighty queer things been happenin' down there lately. A fisherman I know was scared near to death. There's been some peculiar lights around the caves and shootin' too."

"Shooting!" Frank exclaimed.

"Guns goin' off!" the storekeeper said emphatically, as if they had failed to understand him. "Two men already tried to find out what was goin' on there and got shot at."

Frank pricked up his ears. He wondered whether either of these men was Cadmus Quill. The boy described the college assistant to the old fellow and asked if he had seen such a man.

"Naw. These were local citizens. But they won't go back to those caves again, I'll tell you."

Still mumbling his disapproval, Mr Tuttle nonetheless supplied the boys with the provisions they needed. These were packed into the rucksacks which the boys slung over their shoulders.

They returned to the camping site and ate lunch. Then they took down the tent, stowed it into Chet's car, and set off in two vehicles, following the directions the storekeeper had given them.

They retraced their route over the highway, then turned to the right down a steep rutted lane that ended on the open seashore near the fisherman's cottage.

The small house was built at the base of the hill two hundred yards from where the beach ended abruptly against towering cliffs. The waves battered against the sheer wall of rock. The quartet could make out a winding path leading up the hill directly behind the cottage.

"I know what they call this place," Chet said gravely.

"Does it have a name?" Biff asked.

"Sure. Fish Hook."

"Fish Hook? Why?" Biff asked, neatly falling into Chet's trap.

"Because it's at the end of the line." Chet guffawed and slapped Biff on the back.

Biff groaned. "You really hooked me on that one, pal."

"Okay," said Joe. "Let's cut the comedy and see if we can park here."

The boys approached the door of the cottage and knocked. It was opened by a stocky, leather-faced man of middle age. He had a look of surprise on his good-natured countenance.

"Mr John Donachie?" Frank asked.

"Correct. What can I do for you boys?" he inquired.

"May we leave our cars here for a while?" Frank asked.

"Sure. For an hour or so?"

"Perhaps for a few days," Frank replied.

The fisherman's expression changed instantly to one of concern. "You're not goin' over to the caves, are you?"

When Frank said Yes, the man shook his head gravely. "You'd best be goin' back home," he warned. "There's strange doin's in the caves these days. It's no place for boys like you."

The fisherman was joined by his plump, rosy-faced wife who repeated the admonition.

Frank felt his spine tingle. His hunch persisted that Cadmus Quill might be mixed up in the mysterious occurrences at Honeycomb Caves.

"What's been going on there?" Frank pressed.

"Lights mostly and shootin'."

"Haven't any people been seen?"

"Not a livin' soul."

"That's strange," Chet said.

"Strange ain't the word for it," declared the fisherman. "It's downright spooky, like ghosts or somethin'."

"Have you been down to the caves yourself, Mr Donachie?" Frank asked.

"Just call me Johnny." The fisherman said that a few days before, his boat was washed ashore there in a squall. "When I got back in the sea again," he went on, "I saw a couple o' lights down near the caves. Next I heard two or three shots and then a yell."

"A yell?" Frank asked.

"The most awful screechin' I ever heard," the fisherman said.

"Well, that proves *somebody's* there," Biff remarked. Despite the Donachies' warnings, the boys were determined to set out.

"Can you show us the quickest route?" Joe asked.

With a resigned look, the fisherman led the boys a short distance along the beach and pointed to the path leading up the hill. "You'll have to follow that to the top of the cliffs. From there look for a deep ravine. That'll take you down to the caves."

The campers thanked the couple, and with knapsacks and blanket rolls over their shoulders, began the ascent. The hill was steeper than it looked and it was more than an hour before the boys reached the summit.

Here a magnificent view awaited them. Far below lay the fisherman's cottage like a toy house. The ocean was a flat blue floor.

Venturing close to the edge of the cliff, Joe peered over. He saw a sheer wall of rock with a few scrubby outcroppings of gnarled bushes.

"No wonder the caves can't be reached by skirting the shore," Joe said. "The only way along the base of the cliff is by boat."

Chet looked up at the sky. "Come on, fellows," he said. "We can't afford to lose any time. We're in for a storm." The breeze bore to their ears the rumble of distant thunder.

"Chet's right," Joe said. "These squalls come up suddenly. Let's move!"

Without further ado, the boys hastened along the faint trail that led among the rocks. They could see no sign of the ravine, but judged that it would be almost invisible until they came upon it.

A few raindrops hit the faces of the boys as they plodded on. Flashes of lightning zigzagged across the darkening sky, followed by a terrific thunderclap. Then rain started falling heavily.

The wind rose, and far below, the surf boomed and crashed against the base of the cliff. The foursome stumbled on, scarcely able to follow the path in the gloom. The wind howled, lightning flashed, and thunder crashed constantly.

With Frank in the lead, the boys plunged forward into the streaming wall of rain. Chet and Biff were next and Joe brought up the rear. On and on they went, heads bent to the storm. Would they ever find the ravine?

Suddenly Frank came to a stop and looked behind. "Where's Joe?" he shouted above the clamour of the gale. The others looked about. Joe had vanished!

·9·

The Cavern

"WHERE on earth did Joe disappear to?" exclaimed Biff.

He, Frank and Chet peered through the teeming rain, but the gloom was so intense that it was impossible to see more than a few yards away.

"We'll have to go back," Frank decided quickly. "Joe probably sat down to rest and got lost when he tried to catch up with us."

The trio retraced their steps over the rocks, keeping close together. They shouted again and again, but in the roar of the storm they knew there was little chance that Joe would hear them.

"Perhaps he fell down and hurt himself," Biff suggested. "He may be lying behind one of these big rocks where we can't see him."

"Maybe he fell over the cliff!" said Chet, voicing the thought for all of them. For a heartsick moment the boys just stood there, faces pale and streaming with rain. Suddenly, above the roar of the storm, they heard a faint cry.

"Listen!" Frank exclaimed.

Breathlessly, they waited.

Again came the cry. "Help! Help!"

The three boys ran to the edge of the cliff, stopped and peered down. Over to one side, about four feet below, they spied a dark figure.

It was Joe, clinging to a small bush growing out of the sheer cliffside. "Hurry!" he called in a strained voice.

"Hang on! We'll get you!" Frank shouted. But his heart sank when he saw that Joe was beyond his reach.

"There's only one thing to do," he said to Biff and Chet. "You two hang on to me while I lower myself over."

"You'll never make it," Biff protested, as Frank shrugged off the gear he was carrying. "You'll both be killed."

"It's the only chance, and I'm going to take it!" Frank flung himself down and began to edge forward until he was leaning far over the edge. Biff and Chet seized his ankles and braced themselves.

Bit by bit, Frank lowered himself head first. He dared not look down, for he was hanging at a dizzy height. "A little more!" he called out.

He swung lower, gripped Joe's wrists, and secured a tight hold. "Ready, Joe?"

"Okay," was the hoarse reply.

"Haul away!"

Chet and Biff began dragging Frank back. There was a double weight now, but the Hardys' staunch friends were equal to it!

Inch by inch the boys were hauled nearer safety. It seemed ages to Frank before he was over the top again.

At that moment, with his brother just below the rim

of the cliff, Frank felt Joe's wrists slipping from his grasp.

But Chet and Biff scrambled forward and seized Joe's shirt. Together the three pulled him over the edge on to the rocky ground.

For a moment the boys were too exhausted to say a word.

"Boy, that was a narrow squeak!" Chet said solemnly.

"We'll stick closer together after this. How did it happen, Joe?" Frank asked.

"I stopped to tie my bootlace. When I looked up again I couldn't see you at all, so I began to run. I didn't realize I was so near the edge of the cliff. Then some of the rock must have broken off under my feet, because everything gave way and I felt myself falling."

When Frank and Joe had recovered from their gruelling experience, they got to their feet and the adventurers resumed their journey over the rocks. This time no one lagged behind and all stayed well away from the edge of the cliff.

In a short time Frank gave a cry of relief. "The ravine!" he yelled.

Through the pouring rain, just a few yards ahead, the others discerned a deep cut in the rocks, and they all scrambled down into it.

Far below, they could dimly see the beach and the breaking rollers. Slipping and stumbling, the Bay-porters made their way down the steep, winding ravine.

Joe was first to reach bottom.

"Look! A cave!" He pointed right towards the base of the cliff. There, but a short distance from the breaking waves, was a dark hole in the steep wall of rock.

Frank took a flashlight from his pack and led the way into the dark mouth of the cavern. In its gleam he saw that their shelter was no mere niche in the face of the cliff, but a cave that led to unknown depths.

"Looks as if we can start exploring right here and now," he said.

"Explore my neck!" grumbled Chet. "Let's build a fire. I'm wet clear through!"

"What do we do for firewood?" practical Biff inquired.

This had not occurred to the others. They glanced at one another in dismay.

"That's right," Joe said. "There's not much wood around and it's soaked by now, anyway."

Frank moved farther back into the dark cave with his flashlight. Suddenly he exclaimed in mingled astonishment and delight. "Well! Can you beat this, fellows?"

"What?" called Joe.

"Firewood!"

"Where?"

The others came hastening over to Frank.

"Look!" He cast the flashlight beam against the cave wall to his left.

In the centre of the circle of radiance, they saw a neat pile of wood.

Joe whistled in surprise. "That didn't get here by accident—someone stacked it."

Frank stepped over and picked up one of the sticks. "Good dry driftwood. We'll have a roaring fire now."

"I wonder who piled it in here," Biff remarked.

Chet shrugged. "Why worry about that?"

"Probably the mystery men who are doing all the yelling and shooting," Biff said. "We'll be in for it if this is *their* cave we've stumbled on."

He, Chet and Joe began carrying wood over to the centre of the cave. Frank, meanwhile, set down the flashlight, took out his pocketknife, and whittled a particularly dry stick until he had a small heap of shavings. Over these he built a pyramid of driftwood. Then he took a match from his waterproof case and ignited the shavings. They flared up brightly.

Anxiously the boys watched the small blaze. Frank had been afraid that lack of a draught might cause so much smoke that they would be almost suffocated. To his relief, the smoke spiralled upwards and was carried off. "Must be an opening in the roof," Frank observed.

Soon the fire was burning briskly. As its warmth penetrated the cave, the boys took off their drenched clothes and spread them about the blaze, then wrapped themselves in the heavy blankets they had brought with them.

The rest of the afternoon the rain continued un-abated. The clothes dried slowly. Once Biff went to the cave mouth and looked out at the wind-lashed sea.

"Do you think the water comes in here at high tide?" he asked.

"No," Frank replied. "The cave floor was dry when we came."

At dusk Chet produced the frying pan, and the fragrant odour of sizzling bacon soon permeated their refuge. The boys never enjoyed a meal more than their supper in the cave. The driftwood blazed and crackled, casting a cheerful glow which illuminated the rocky ceiling and walls of the underground chamber. With crisp bacon, bread toasted brown before the fire, hot chocolate, and jam, they ate ravenously, and at last sat back with deep sighs of sheer content.

Although part of the floor of the cave was rocky, much of it was sand, which provided a fairly comfortable resting-place. The boys were tired after their long journey, so they stretched out in their blankets and were soon drowsily chatting, while the fire died lower and lower. At last it was only a glow in the dark and the voices ceased.

An hour passed. Two hours.

Suddenly Joe was awakened. He was just about to turn over and go to sleep again, wondering vaguely what had aroused him, when he heard a footstep close by.

He raised himself on one elbow and peered into the gloom, but could see nothing.

When he heard a rustle, he spoke up. "Is that you, Frank?" The words rang out clearly in the deep silence.

Instead of the reassuring voice of his brother, Joe heard a muffled exclamation and scurrying footsteps. Someone was running across the floor of the cave!

·10·

A Terrifying Loss

"Who's that?" demanded Joe, scrambling to his feet.

There was no answer.

"Fellows! Wake up!" Joe exclaimed, as he stumbled about in the darkness, trying to find his flashlight.

"What's the matter?" came Chet's sleepy voice. "It isn't morning yet. Let me sleep."

"Wake up! Someone's prowling around here."

"Maybe it was Biff," came Frank's voice. "Biff, you here?"

There was a deep sigh. Then Biff said drowsily, "Of course I am, why?"

Frank switched on his flashlight and played the beam around the cave. Biff and Chet sat up in their blankets and blinked. "What's wrong?" Biff demanded.

Joe told about the intruder.

"Did he go out the front way?" Biff asked.

Joe shook his head. "No. He seemed to go farther into the cave."

"Well, then," Frank said decisively, "we'll go and look for him."

The boys hurriedly dressed, and taking flashlights, followed Frank deeper into the stygian cave. Thirty paces ahead they were confronted by an arch in the rock, an opening that seemed to lead into a tunnel. They walked into it cautiously, and Frank kept his light focused on the floor to make sure no pitfalls lay before them.

The tunnel was about fifteen feet in length and six feet high. As the floor was of solid rock, they were unable to find any footprints indicating that someone had passed that way.

The tunnel led to another cave. "Maybe there's a regular chain of caves!" Joe exclaimed as the boys stepped out into a massive underground chamber.

"I guess ours is only the beginning," Chet remarked.

In the glow of their flashlights the foursome saw that the huge room in which they now stood had a number of dark openings in the walls. These were, presumably, tunnels leading into caves beyond.

Frank frowned. "There are at least a dozen different passages out of here. The prowler might have taken any of them."

"Let's tackle the biggest," Biff suggested.

"Good idea. If we don't get anywhere, we'll try the others."

The largest tunnel was straight ahead. The boys crossed the cavern and Frank led them into the dark passage. Seconds later he exclaimed softly, "Look!"

"What?"

"A footprint."

Clearly discernible was the imprint of a boot in a patch of wet sand.

"We're on the right trail," Joe said quietly. "Come on!"

With increasing excitement, the searchers pressed

forward and in a few moments emerged into another cave. This was an enormous underground vault, the largest they had yet seen. Even the four flashlight beams failed to reveal all of the rocky walls and ceiling.

As they started to cross it, Biff's light went out. He muttered in annoyance and tried to coax a gleam from the silvery tube. No luck.

"Take mine," Frank offered, but Biff declined. "Stay close, then," Frank said, as they continued across the huge cavern.

The floor of the cavern was piled high with rocks, evidently from cave-ins over the years. In other parts it was pitted with gullies and holes. In trying to avoid these, the boys gradually became separated.

Biff stumbled along behind. He felt the loss of his flashlight, but said nothing, relying on the radiance provided by the others.

Soon, however, the three lights became widely scattered. Biff found himself in total darkness.

He stood uncertainly for a moment, then called out, "Hey, fellows, wait for me!"

He took a step forward and stumbled. As he fell, he groped wildly for a firm rock, but there was nothing there.

With a cry of terror, Biff hurtled down into blackness.

For a moment the other three boys froze in their tracks. Then they shouted for Biff, time and again, but there was no answer. They searched frantically among the rocks and crevices, but found no sign of him.

In the glow of the flashlights they looked at one another anxiously and listened in vain for a faint cry.

There was no sound but the echoes of their own voices.

"We won't give up!" Frank vowed. "We'll search every pit and hole in here!"

With desperate patience they scoured the cave, but at last were forced to admit that it was no use.

"This place is too big," Chet said dejectedly. "We need more light." He sat down on a rock and buried his face in his hands.

"I have an idea," Frank offered. "Let's build a fire. That'll help."

Chet brightened. "Good idea!"

"Come on," Frank said. "We have lots of wood left in the outside cave."

"That's not a bad stunt!" Joe declared hopefully. "With a roaring bonfire we'll be able to light up the whole place enough to see what we're doing."

The boys retraced their steps into the outer cavern where they had slept. They filled their arms with wood and were about to re-enter the tunnel when Joe noticed something that made him drop his wood on the stone floor with a clatter.

"What's wrong?" Chet asked.

"That's funny," Joe returned. "I was sure we left our supplies right near this woodpile."

"We did," Frank assured him.

Joe turned his flashlight on the place where the greater part of their supplies had been stacked. A loaf of bread and a tin of sardines lay on the rock, but that was all.

"They've been stolen!" Frank exclaimed.

"By that prowler, I'll bet!" Joe said. "He probably

hid himself until we passed, then sneaked back here and stole our food."

"We can't worry about that now," Frank said grimly. "Let's go!"

Swiftly Joe gathered up his firewood and the boys returned to the big vault.

Hastily the fire was built and soon the flames flared high. The companions were surprised at the number of holes and crevices now revealed.

"It's a wonder we weren't all killed," Chet said. "We were prowling around this chamber without any idea of the real danger."

Methodically the boys resumed their search, investigating each opening, deep or shallow. But in spite of the extra light and all their shouting, their efforts were in vain.

"I'm afraid it's no use," Chet said, gulping. "It's as if Biff was swallowed up."

"We need help," Frank said tersely. "We'll go to the village and get some men with ropes and searchlights."

Disconsolately the boys turned back. But as they did, Chet let out a bloodcurdling cry.

On the wall of the cavern flickered the huge shadow of a hand!

·11·

No Trespassing!

THE ghostly shadow caused the boys' hearts to pound until they saw the reason for it. A hand was reaching up from one of the pits, and the bonfire's glow threw its silhouette on the cavern wall.

"Biff!" Joe cried out.

Only a groan answered. The Hardys and Chet leaped towards the faltering hand as it groped for the lip of the pit. Frank grasped it and together the boys pulled Biff out. He lay dazed for a moment.

"You're hurt!" said Joe, bending down to examine a large egg on Biff's left temple.

"I'm all right now. A little dizzy yet, but it isn't serious."

"What happened?"

"I fell into the pit and struck my head against the rocks. When I came to, I was lying beneath an overhang. I must have been out for a few minutes."

"A few minutes!" Chet exclaimed. "We've been hunting for you for over an hour."

Biff looked incredulous and shook his head in dismay when told about the stolen supplies.

"Boy! What a mess we're in," he said, as his companions helped him out of the cavern.

They returned to the outer cave and fell fast asleep. When morning came, a diligent inspection of their quarters failed to reveal any clues as to the thief.

"We're out of luck, that's all," Frank concluded. "Our light-fingered friend fooled us neatly."

"At least the storm is over," said Biff, who was feeling better.

From the cave they could see the sun shining on the blue waters of the sea. As Chet unlimbered his metal detector he moved it over a rocky part of the floor. "Hmm. That's funny," he said.

"Did you find a pirate's chest?" Joe grinned.

"No. But I hear a buzzing noise. Maybe this thing's broken." He moved outside and began to swing the disc back and forth over the beach.

All at once Chet dropped his detector, fell to his knees, and dug furiously in the sand. His astonished companions watched from the cave entrance.

Finally the stout boy pulled something out and held it aloft in his right hand. "Ha! I told you!" he shouted.

"What is it?" Biff asked, as he, Frank and Joe hurried over.

"A pistol. Probably a pirate's. Or maybe from the sunken ship."

"By golly, Chet, I have to hand it to you," said Frank, as he examined the piece and wiped wet sand from it. "Hey, wait! This isn't old."

"You're right!" Joe burst in. "It's hardly rusted at all." He handled the weapon. "Looks like a Smith and Wesson."

"But see the marking," Biff said. "Made in Spain."

Chet looked wisely at his companions. "What do you make of it, boys?"

"Perhaps this very pistol caused all the shooting we've heard about," Biff offered.

Chet beamed. "Well, fellows, I guess *I* found a mystery. Want to solve it?"

"And leave the trail of Todd and Quill?" Joe asked. "Nothing doing!"

"Just a minute," Frank put in. "How do we know Cadmus Quill didn't drop the pistol?"

"Wow!" Joe clapped a hand to his forehead. "That's a pretty wild guess for you, brother."

"You're dreaming, Frank!" Chet chimed in.

Biff, too, thought Frank's guess was farfetched, and added, "Enough of deductions. How about some chow? I'm famished." He looked hopefully up the ravine, but Chet, for once, was more excited about detecting than eating.

"Please, fellows," he begged, "let's go a little way up the beach yet. Who knows what I'll find!"

"Okay," Frank agreed. "Only a quarter of a mile. Then we turn back."

The sandy shore wound about the face of a great bluff of black rock, and when the boys had skirted this precipice they were confronted by a dark opening at the base of the cliff just a few yards away.

"Another cave!" Frank exclaimed.

Chet gave a cheer and ran ahead with his detector.

When they were just in front of the entrance the boys halted with exclamations of surprise.

Tacked on a board stuck in the sand beside the cave mouth was a tattered sheet of paper. Scrawled in heavy black letters were the warning words *No Trespassing*.

The companions looked at the sign in astonishment, then Chet grinned. "By order of the Rockaway chief of police, no doubt. Maybe somebody put it here for a joke," he said. "Let's take a peep inside."

Frank was first to reach the cave and peer inside. Then he turned back to the others. "This sign isn't a joke," he said quietly. "Somebody does live here!"

Curiously the boys crowded into the mouth of the cave. In the gloom they could see a crude table and a mattress with blankets. On a ledge of rock was an improvised cupboard consisting of an old soap carton containing canned goods and other provisions.

"Well," Chet declared, "we have a neighbour who might offer us some grub."

"We certainly have," Biff said, looking down the beach. "And if I'm not mistaken, here he comes now."

Along the shore strode a tall, grey-haired man wearing a blue shirt and overalls, the legs of which were tucked into high rubber boots. The man, oblivious to the boys, held a bugle in his left hand. He stopped, looked at the sea, and blew a loud, clear call. Then he wiped his lips with the back of his hand and continued towards the cave.

When he spotted the four boys he stopped short, blew another flurry on the bugle, and hastened up to the Bayporters.

"I'm Commander E. K. T. Wilson, Queen's Navy, retired," he announced. "You should have saluted, but I guess you didn't know."

To make up for this breach of etiquette, the boys

saluted smartly. This appeared to gratify the man immensely.

"You're landlubbers, eh?"

"I suppose so," Frank admitted with a smile.

"Well, we can't all be sailors. It isn't often people come to see me."

"Do you live here?" Joe asked, indicating the cave.

"This is my home when I'm ashore. I'm resting between cruises just now. What are your names?"

The boys introduced themselves.

"Glad to meet you," returned Commander Wilson. "I get used to being alone, but it's a pleasure to have visitors."

"It's lonely enough here," Frank agreed.

"Isn't bad. Not half as lonely as the time I got marooned in the South Seas."

The boys looked at him with new interest.

"You were really marooned?" Chet asked.

"Aye. It was when I was in command of a destroyer cruising the South Seas a good many years ago. We landed for water on a little island that you won't find on any map. It was a hot day—very hot. Must have been over a hundred degrees in the shade. So while my men were loading the water on my ship I sat down in the shade of a cactus tree. Before I knew it, I was asleep."

"And they went away and left you?" Joe put in.

"They did."

"But you were the captain!"

"I guess they thought I was in my cabin, and of course none of 'em dared disturb me. When I woke up, the ship was gone."

"Ee-yow!" Biff exclaimed.

"Well, sir, I didn't know what to do. I was like this here fellow Robinson Crusoe that you read about. But I had to make the best of it, so I fixed myself up a little house and lived there for nearly six months, all by myself."

"Didn't the ship come back for you?"

"They couldn't find the island again. Anyway, the quartermaster who took charge of the ship didn't want to find me, I guess. He wanted my job."

"Did you have anything to eat on the island?" Biff asked.

Chet interrupted. "Speaking of food, Commander, could you help us out with some breakfast?"

"Sure, me hearties. Growing boys should eat plenty. Now what was I talking about? Oh, well, doesn't matter."

A wink passed around the circle of friends as the man went inside and returned with a slab of bacon. Chet volunteered to start a fire, and got it going quickly as the old man cut strips of bacon and put them into a frying pan.

"How about a swim while we're waiting?" Frank suggested.

"Let's go!" Joe shouted.

The boys skinned off their clothes and ran into the surf. Joe swam beside his brother. "Frank, Wilson doesn't sound much like an Englishman."

"I don't think he has all his marbles," Frank replied.

"Do you think Wilson helped himself to our supplies?"

"I didn't see them in his cave," Frank said, adding,

"He seems harmless. I'd like to ask him some questions, though."

"And could I go for some crisp bacon! Race you back to shore!"

Using the Australian crawl, the brothers streaked over the wave tops and hit shore together. There Biff and Chet joined them, and after they dressed, the refreshed quartet trotted up to Commander Wilson, who sat near the fire. The frying pan lay at the sailor's side—empty, and Wilson was chewing on the last piece of bacon. He looked up.

"Who are you?" he asked bluntly.

"The Hardy boys," Frank began in surprise. "And what—"

"Well, beat it! Scram! I don't want you around here!"

·12·

Undercover Work

COMMANDER WILSON's gruff order to leave caused the four boys to stare at him in wonderment.

"But, Commander," Joe protested, "you—"

"Don't 'Commander' me!" the man said, rising to his feet and shaking his fist at the boys. "I want to be left alone! That's why I'm a hermit."

Frank shook his head. "No use arguing, fellows," he murmured. "Come on."

They strode away across the sand, with Chet muttering about the loss of a good meal.

"That old sailor's a real lulu," Biff said, disgruntled. He glanced at Frank. "What'll we do now?"

"First thing is to get some food."

"And where is the food?" Biff asked sarcastically.

"Maybe we can grow mushrooms in the cave," Joe quipped.

Chet trailed behind. The headphones were clamped to his ears, and once more he swung his metal detector back and forth over the sand.

"If you have strength enough," Frank told Biff, "we can climb up the ravine, cross the cliffs, and go back down to Johnny the fisherman's place. Maybe he'll give

THE SECRET OF THE CAVES 91

us chow, or else we can drive back to Rockaway for
more supplies."

"Bright prospects!" Biff grumbled. "I thought I
could do some fishing today. It's great after a storm."
Then suddenly Biff recalled that his fishing gear
had been stolen with the rucksacks. "Doggone it!"
he exclaimed. "That burns me up! I'll bet that Commander Wilson took our stuff and stashed it out of
sight!"

"I doubt it," Frank said. He turned and called to
Chet, who was now a hundred paces behind. "Come
on, hurry up!"

Chet waved and nodded, but still continued to swing
his detector. Then he gave an excited bellow.

"Sounds like the mating call of a walrus," Biff commented.

"He may have discovered another weapon," Joe said,
as they hastened back to their stout pal.

"Hey, fellows, there must be a whole arsenal underneath here," Chet said. "You should have heard the
terrific noise in my ears."

All four boys dropped to their hands and knees and
dug like fox-terriers in a bone yard. Biff was first to
reach something solid. He tugged and yanked, finally
coming up with a rucksack!

"Look!" Biff cried out. "It's mine!" He brushed the
wet sand from the knapsack, opened it quickly, and
pulled out his collapsible fishing gear.

The other three quickly recovered their supplies, a
little damp, but none the worse for their burial in
sand.

Chet unscrewed the lid of his canteen and took a

long swallow of water. "I told you this metal detector would pay off," he said.

Biff grinned. "I could kiss you, Chet, for finding my tackle."

Chet stepped backwards in mock horror. "Please, please, not here," he said, and the others roared with laughter.

As their own cave was not far from the spot, the boys hastened back and took out the rations. A fire was quickly started and Chet presided over the frying pan filled with crisp bacon. "Phooey on the commander," Chet said smugly.

"Which reminds me," Frank put in, "I'm not finished with that old codger yet."

"What more could you learn from him?" Joe asked. "He's as nutty as a fruitcake."

"Maybe he is, maybe he isn't," Frank replied. "In either case, I'd like to study him a little closer and ask some more questions."

Joe looked thoughtful as he spooned a portion of scrambled eggs into his tin plate. "Do you think he might have seen Cadmus Quill or some other mysterious prowlers around here?"

As Frank broke off a piece of crusty bread from a long loaf, he said that was exactly his idea.

"Well, you fellows go about your sleuthing," Biff said. "I'm going fishing."

"Where?" asked Chet.

"From the top of the cliff," Biff replied. "I can heave my line a mile out from that point. Maybe I'll catch something big where the water's deep."

"I'm with you," Chet said. He turned to the Hardys

and added, "If you fellows run into trouble with Wilson, just call us."

During the rest of the meal the boys talked about the thief who had buried their supplies in the sand.

"If he didn't keep them for his own use, what was the point of stealing 'em?" Biff mused.

"To get us away from here," Joe said promptly. "Somebody doesn't want us around."

"Like Commander Wilson," Biff said. "What do you think, Frank?"

The young sleuth shrugged. "There might be one man or two—maybe a whole gang operating around here. But we'll find out sooner or later."

"You'd better find out sooner," Chet declared, "else we'll be starving again."

"If you mean somebody's going to steal our supplies a second time," Joe said, "you're mistaken." He told of having seen a small crevice fifty yards away at the base of the ravine. "We'll hide our stuff there until you two get back with the whale you're going to catch."

When the fire had been put out and their camping place tidied up, the four adventurers hid their rucksacks and parted.

Frank glanced over his shoulder to see Chet and Biff trudging up the ravine, as he and Joe trotted towards Wilson's cave. They saw the old sailor standing in front of his cave, sketching something in the sand with a slender stick. When he saw them approach, he quickly rubbed the sole of his boot over the sand and hailed the brothers. "Hello there! Have you come to visit me?"

Frank and Joe exchanged glances, and walked up to the man. "Why, yes," said Frank. "Do you remember us, Frank and Joe Hardy?"

"Of course I do. Where did you go after I invited you to breakfast?"

"Why, we came—" Frank began.

"Didn't see hide nor hair of you. Thought you went back to Bayhill, or Portside, or wherever you came from. Where are your two friends?"

"They went fishing," Joe replied.

"Where?"

"To the top of the cliffs."

"Dangerous. Mighty dangerous. I hope they come back all right," Wilson said.

He shook his head, clasped his hands behind his back, and walked in circles before his cave.

"Commander Wilson," Frank began slowly, "have you seen any people prowling around Honeycomb Caves?"

Wilson stopped short and looked Frank squarely in the eyes. "I'm alone. A hermit. That's what I am. I haven't seen anybody. Nobody comes near me. They think I'm queer."

Joe described both Todd and Quill. "Have you seen anyone resembling them?" he persisted.

"No. But come to think of it, there *was* a fellow—"

The Hardys looked alertly at the old sailor. Had he seen one of the missing men?

"Yes, go on," Frank encouraged. "What did he look like?"

"The first one you mentioned."

"Todd?"

"Yes. I once knew a fellow like that. He was second mate on my cruiser in the Philippines."

Joe turned aside and made a wry face as the man continued:

"Come to think of it, his name was Todd. Yes, it was," the commander went on. "He shipwrecked me deliberately and I had to climb a pineapple tree until the natives stopped beating their drums and went home."

Joe leaned close to Frank and said in a low voice, "He's off again. What'll we do now?"

As Commander Wilson rambled on, Frank edged closer to the mouth of the cave and glanced inside. He gave an involuntary start as he saw something he had not noticed before. But before he could whisper to Joe, Wilson wheeled about. "A man's cave is his castle," he said tartly.

Frank tried to manage a grin. "Well, I guess we'd better be going, Commander," he said. "Those fellows must have caught a fish by now."

Without saying a word, the old salt went into his cave. The Hardys continued down the beach again. When they had gone a dozen yards, Frank seized Joe's arm and pulled him behind a large rock.

"What's the matter, Frank?"

"Joe, I saw a cap in Wilson's cave—the same foreign style that was dropped by the fellow at the radar site!"

"Do you think there's some connection?"

Frank suggested that they hide and watch the old fellow's cave. "You notice he got mighty excited when I looked into his quarters."

"I'll bet he's got something in there he doesn't want us to see," he said, peering over the rock. Suddenly he hissed, "Watch it! Here he comes!"

The two boys crouched low. Joe poked his head around the boulder for a quick look. "Frank, he's going down the beach the other way—probably to look in our cave."

"Now's our chance to explore his," Frank said. "Is he out of sight yet?"

"Yes."

Frank and Joe scrambled out of their hiding-place and dashed into Wilson's cave.

"Boy, is it deep!" Joe exclaimed. "It goes away back!"

"And look here," Frank said, picking up the cap from the floor. "This could be more than a coincidence."

"Wow! He's got an arsenal too!" whispered Joe. He pointed to a shotgun lying on a rock ledge.

"So that's where the mysterious shooting came from," Frank guessed. "And how about this?"

He picked up a dog-eared notebook from beside the gun and leafed through it.

"It's a code book! Let's take it to the light so we can study it."

The boys had been well schooled in cryptography by their father. Eagerly the two moved nearer the mouth of the cave.

All at once the interior darkened and Commander Wilson stood at the entrance! "Spies! You're all spies!" he boomed. "Give me that book, you—you young pirates!"

As Frank and Joe stood tongue-tied, Wilson lunged towards the stone ledge.

"Look out!" Joe cried out. "He's going for the shotgun!"

· 13 ·

A Straight-Line Clue

FRANK dropped the code book and leaped to intercept Commander Wilson before he could reach the shotgun. But the old man was as agile as an athlete! He dodged and twisted out of Frank's way like a piece of spring steel and grabbed the weapon.

"Frank! Run!" Joe shouted, as he ducked towards the front of the cave.

Realizing it was now impossible to cope with Wilson, Frank dashed after his brother. But as the two boys reached the cave mouth, there was a loud explosion. Frank stumbled and fell to the ground.

"You killed him! You killed my brother!" Joe cried out. He bent down over the prostrate form. But instead of finding blood on the back of Frank's red shirt, Joe saw a large, round white patch. At the same time Frank shook his head, got to his knees, then stood up.

"Are you all right?" Joe asked. Out of the corner of his eye he saw the smoking shotgun in Wilson's hand. The old man had a gleeful expression on his face.

"I'm okay," Frank said. "Let's get out of here!"

The boys retreated halfway to the water's edge before stopping.

"The blast knocked me down," Frank said, reaching about gingerly to touch his back. "What was the gun loaded with?" He removed his shirt and the brothers examined it closely. "Joe! This looks like flour! It *is* flour!"

"So that's what Wilson used for ammunition!" Joe said. "Now I know for sure he's off his head."

With mixed feelings of embarrassment and chagrin, Frank donned his shirt and the Hardys looked back as Wilson emerged from the cave. Again he shook his fist.

"That's what you spies get for snooping around Commander Wilson's cave!" he shouted. "You have some nerve trying to read the code book of the Queen's Navy!"

"We were only looking at that funny cap," Frank called back. "Where did you get it?"

"In Rockaway, of course—where I get all my supplies," Wilson said. "That's where I go when the Queen's Navy forgets to send the supply ship."

Shaken by the weird incident, the brothers headed for their cave.

"That cap will bear some investigating," said Joe.

"You're right," Frank agreed. "If they're sold at the general store in Rockaway, maybe the Bayport prowler bought his there too."

"Look who's coming," said Joe. They glanced up to see Chet and Biff scrambling down the ravine towards them. Biff had a monster of a fish slung across his shoulder.

"Hi, fellows!" Chet called out. "Look what we caught!"

Joe grinned. "It's almost as good as a whale!"

Puffing and beaming, Chet and Biff hastened up to the Hardys. The sea bass which Biff carried weighed more than thirty pounds.

"Will we stuff ourselves today!" Chet said gleefully, then added quickly, "And I discovered a mine, too."

"A gold mine, I suppose," Joe said.

"I don't know what kind," Chet said seriously, "but my detector picked up some funny noises."

"Chet's right," Biff said. "*Something's* buried up there. Fellows, you ought to go and hear for yourselves. I'll show you the place."

"Okay. You win," Frank said sceptically.

"I'll cook some of the fish while you're gone," Chet said. He added wistfully, "I wish we had some flour to sprinkle on it."

Frank gulped and Joe pounded him on the back.

"Did I say something wrong?" Chet asked.

"Oh, no!" Frank said hastily. "Give us the detector, Chet."

Joe took the device and in a few minutes the three boys were clambering up the ravine towards the top of the cliff.

When they reached it, Joe donned the earphones and held the detector several inches off the ground. "Over there," Biff directed. Joe went towards the spot. A moment later he winced as a clicking chattered like a machine-gun in his ears.

"No kidding, there is something underneath here," he said. "Listen for yourself, Frank."

Frank complied, then moved the detector from right to left. "That's strange," he muttered. "This mine, or whatever it is Chet discovered, runs in a straight line."

"Maybe a water pipe," Biff said. "Wouldn't that be a joke!"

"A water pipe from where to where?" Joe countered. "Why put a drain underground at a place like this?"

"Whatever the thing is," Frank said, "it lies east to west, apparently from near the coastline to the highway."

"I've got an idea," Joe said. He moved to a clump of pine trees growing several hundred yards back from the precipice and selected the tallest. "Give me a boost, Frank."

After getting a lift from his brother, Joe shinned to the first branch, scrambled to the top of the tree, and looked intently westward.

"What do you see over there?" Frank called up.

"You'd be surprised!" said Joe.

"Come on," Biff said. "You're tracing an imaginary line. What does it point to?"

"The Palais Paris," Joe replied. In a few moments he was back on the ground. "Frank, I have a strange feeling about that place. Let's investigate it."

"Not this minute," his brother replied. "I'd like to do some digging."

"But with what?" asked Joe.

"I'll get some tools," Biff volunteered. "Johnny the fisherman will lend us his." He hastened off and returned presently with a shovel and pick-axe over his shoulder.

The boys took turns at wielding the pick and shovel. Rocks and dirt flew up out of the hole they fashioned. But they reached three feet down without striking metal.

Biff leaned on the shovel and ran his thumb along his brow like a windscreen wiper. "We might dig all day and not find anything," he said. "Frank, do you suppose it *is* a metallic substance which makes the detector click like that?"

"I'm not sure," Frank replied. "It might be an electrical conduit. Let's check in Rockaway."

"Okay." Joe chuckled. "As soon as we've eaten that feast Chet's preparing for us."

The boys left the tools near the edge of the cliff where they could find them, then retreated down the ravine to the cave. Chet had made a spit, on which large chunks of the freshly caught sea bass were grilling over hot coals.

"Smells great, Chet," Joe said. "Let's eat and be on our way."

"We're going back?" Chet asked in dismay.

"To Rockaway for the time being," said Frank, and told what they had observed on the cliff-top.

"Then I did find a good clue, eh?" Chet asked proudly. "First the pistol and now this. What would you fellows do without me?"

"We'll make an operator out of you, like Dad's assistant, Sam Radley," Frank said.

"Just so long as it isn't dangerous," Chet said, and passed out portions of the succulent fish. Frank, Joe and Biff had to admit it was one of the finest meals they had ever tasted.

"It's great brain food," said Chet. "I think we're going to need it on this case of yours," he added with a wink at the Hardys.

"Don't worry," Biff said. "They'll get to the bottom of this—some day."

The banter flew back and forth until the meal was finished. Then Chet put out the fire and the boys packed for the return trip. Camping in the salty sea air seemed to give them extra energy. They sang their way along the top of the cliff, where they picked up the digging tools and made the long descent to the fisherman's house.

Mrs Donachie came out to greet them. "Oh, I'm so glad all you boys returned safely from those awful caves," she said.

"We're still in one piece." Joe grinned. "Is Johnny here? We're returning his tools."

"He's out fishing," the woman said. "I'll tell him you stopped by."

The boys said goodbye and headed for their cars. "Come back when you please," Mrs Donachie called after them.

The Bayporters waved goodbye and drove quickly back to Rockaway, where they pulled up in front of the general store. Frank led the way inside.

Mr Tuttle, the proprietor, was sitting behind the counter, his chair tipped back. "Well, what did I tell you?" he greeted them, shaking his head vigorously. "You got into trouble at the caves, so you came back!"

"Who said anything about trouble?" Chet demanded.

"Well, you've got somethin' on your minds." The

whiskered man squinted. "I can tell by the way you barged in here."

"To tell you the truth," Frank said, "we have. I wonder if you could direct us to the town engineer's office. We'd like to study some public maps and surveys."

The old fellow raised himself expansively and snapped his braces. "Seein' that I'm the mayor of Rockaway," he said, "I can show you to the archives." With a flourish of his right hand, he indicated a door at the back of the store.

"In there?" asked Joe.

"That's the office of the mayor *and* the town engineer," the storekeeper said.

The boys followed him into the room. To their surprise they found it neatly arranged, with a desk, a filing cabinet, and large survey maps on the walls. These showed the adjoining countryside, complete with service lines of all kinds.

Frank and Joe studied the maps carefully as Biff and Chet looked over their shoulders.

"No, I can't see any electrical conduits or water pipes," said Frank as his finger followed the area from the cliffs to the Palais Paris. "Joe, you may have a good hunch about that place. I've got an idea."

When Mayor Tuttle asked about their interest in the maps, Frank deftly turned the question aside, saying what a good camping site they had in Rockaway.

After buying more supplies, the boys drove to the camping site.

"Hey, Frank, what's this big idea of yours?" Joe asked impatiently.

Frank grinned. "Gather round and listen. It may work." He said that Joe and Chet would be dispatched to Bayport, while he and Biff continued sleuthing in Rockaway. "Your mission," he told his brother, "will be to get Callie and Iola to apply for waitress jobs at the Palais Paris."

·14·

Startling News

JOE whistled. "A great idea, Frank. The girls can be our undercover agents."

"Exactly," Frank said. He turned to Chet. "Maybe you can convince Iola she should do this for Hardy and Sons."

"I think she'd do it just for Joe," Chet said, and guffawed.

"All right, all right," Joe said, "let's go." He called over his shoulder. "Find out about that cap, Frank!"

He and Chet hopped into the jalopy and drove away. Two hours later they pulled into the driveway of the Morton farmhouse.

Iola and Mary Todd hastened out to greet them. Mary, although happy to see the boys, had a wistful air. Joe realized she was disappointed that her brother had not been found, and wished he had good news for her.

When the four young people had gathered in the cool spacious living-room, Joe asked Iola, "Will you get Callie Shaw to come right over?"

"I'll phone her now. Why?"

"Tell you later."

While they waited for Callie, tall frosty glasses of lemonade were served by Iola, who grew more curious with each cool sip. Twenty minutes later Callie Shaw arrived. She was a good-looking blonde girl whom Frank Hardy often dated.

"Hi, everybody," she said, her eyes sparkling. "Why the mysterious summons?"

"Yes, Joe Hardy," Iola put in. "Don't keep us in suspense any longer.

With a dramatic gesture Joe began. "We have something exceptional to ask you girls."

"I know! You want us to go on a picnic at the caves," Callie said hopefully.

Joe shook his head. "We want you and Iola to apply for waitress jobs at the Palais Paris."

"So you can spy on what's going on there," Chet burst in.

Dumbfounded, the three girls listened intently to the story of the boys' adventures.

"You mean you want us to help you on a detective case?" Iola said happily. "Oh, we'd love to!"

A determined look crossed Mary's pretty face. "If Callie and Iola are going to help you boys find *my* brother, I want to help too."

"But—but—" Chet started to protest.

"No buts about it," Mary said emphatically. "All three of us girls will be detectives!"

Mary's enthusiasm amused Joe and Chet. But Callie and Iola were delighted to have her join them in applying for waitress jobs at the Palais Paris.

"We'll call ourselves the three musketeers!" Iola said proudly.

"Ugh!" said Chet. "I can just see you now duelling with steak knives."

Iola gave her brother a withering look, then turned to Joe with a bright smile. "What do you want us to do when we get there? Shall we go under assumed names?"

"To answer your second question first," said Joe. "You and Callie give your names, but I don't think Mary should use her last one—just in case these people have read about her brother's disappearance."

"All right," Mary said promptly. "I'll call myself Mary Temple."

"Good," Joe replied. "In answer to your first question, Iola—if and when you get to be waitresses, just keep your ears and eyes open for anything suspicious going on at the Palais Paris."

"And not too much giggling either," Chet said, with a brotherly wave of his hand.

"Of course not, silly!" Iola retorted. "When do we start?"

"First thing tomorrow," Joe said. "We'll meet here at eight o'clock."

"Meantime"—Iola's eyes twinkled—"we gals can practise balancing trays."

Afterwards, Joe rode to Bayport with Callie in her sports car. "I'll pick you up in the morning," she said, pulling up at the Hardy home. " 'Bye, now."

Joe was disappointed to learn that his father was out of town. "Your dad won't be back until sometime tomorrow," said Mrs Hardy. "By the way, did you boys find a spinning-wheel?"

"Well—er—yes," Joe replied. "But it needs a little work. We'll fix it up, though, Mom." He added apprehensively, "Aunt Gertrude hasn't arrived yet?"

"No, but I expect her any day."

Joe quickly briefed his mother on their recent adventures, including the cap clue and the plan to return to Rockaway. "There's a phone at the general store in case you want to reach us," he said. Joe had supper and retired early. Right after breakfast he took enough money from the brothers' safe to cover the balance on the spinning-wheel and retrieve Frank's watch.

Promptly at eight o'clock Joe and Callie arrived at the Morton farm, and the five young people set off in Chet's jalopy. Iola sat next to Joe as the teenagers drove happily along the highway to Rockaway.

Frank and Biff met them at the camping site, somewhat surprised to see Mary Todd.

"I have news for you," Frank said. "Old Man Tuttle doesn't sell those foreign caps."

"I told you Wilson was nutty," Joe commented.

It was then decided that Biff should drive the three girls to the restaurant. Frank explained, "The Palais Paris people already know Joe and me. They might get suspicious if we show up with you."

"Well, I don't see why we girls can't drive alone," said Iola. "We have our licences with us."

Although the Hardys knew that Callie and Iola were good drivers, they insisted that Biff go along as a precautionary measure.

"There may be a bunch of gangsters hiding out there," Chet quipped. "And Biff can take care of *them*, eh pal?"

"Single-handed!"

"And don't forget—you are Mary *Temple*," Joe emphasized. The girls waved as Biff drove them away in Chet's car.

"Do you suppose they'll all get jobs?" Joe asked, as he, Frank and Chet watched the car disappear round a bend.

"Even if only one is hired," Frank said, "we'll have an undercover agent on the spot."

"She can always check on those phoney antiques," said Chet, as he pulled up a stalk of grass and nipped it between his teeth. "So, what do we do now?"

The boys were strolling past Tuttle's General Store. Chet answered his own question. "I could go some ice-cream."

"Okay." Joe grinned. "It's hot and we'll have to wait, so why not fuel up, eh, Chet?"

"We can ask Mr Tuttle about Commander Wilson, too," Frank suggested.

Chet treated them to ice-cream on a stick. In between bites, the boys questioned the storekeeper.

"Mr Tuttle," Joe spoke up, "do you know anything about that ex-sailor hermit who lives at the caves? His name is Wilson."

The mayor gave Joe a sideways look. "Hermit? Lives in a cave? Never saw the likes of such in my town, and never heard of a soul *livin'* down there."

The trio said goodbye and left. Chet said, "Let's go to the car. There's a good jazz programme from Bayport."

But as they approached the car, Mayor Tuttle raced out after them. "Hey, come back!" he called excitedly.

"Oh—oh, what now?" said Frank, turning.

The old man went on urgently. "The telephone," he said. "Somebody's calling you—your father."

Frank dashed back inside, followed by Joe and Chet.

He ran to the public booth and picked up the receiver. "Dad, this is Frank. What's up?"

The reply creased a furrow between his eyes. "Leapin' lizards!" he exclaimed. "Okay, Dad. We'll get over there right away. Thanks for calling."

Frank stepped out of the booth, and faced the other boys, who were bursting with curiosity.

"Tell us what happened," Joe demanded.

"Remember that rundown on Cadmus Quill?" Frank said. "Well, Dad learned something else. Guess what—the Palais Paris is owned by a corporation, with Cadmus Quill listed as secretary!"

Joe let out a long whistle. "Then something fishy *is* going on around there," he said. "The girls might be in danger! Let's go!"

Chet sprinted as fast as the Hardys and all three bolted into the car together. Joe spun the rear wheels in his haste to get away!

In the meantime, Iola, Callie and Mary were being ushered through the restaurant of the Palais Paris to the manager's office at the rear. In order to avoid being conspicuous, Biff Hooper had parked Chet's car at the far end of the car-park. Biff himself crouched down out of sight on the floor of the back seat.

The girls were greeted by a suave-looking slender man with a small black moustache. "Mesdemoiselles," he said, rising from his desk, "do I understand that you wish to work as waitresses at the Palais Paris?" The manager spoke with a French accent. He added quickly, "Ah, *pardon*. I am Pierre Dumont."

"Yes, Mr Dumont," Callie Shaw spoke up. "A friend of ours saw your sign. We would like to apply for jobs."

"You speak French?"

"*Oui*," Iola replied. "We've studied it in school."

"*Très bien*." Pierre Dumont nodded. "And you have had restaurant experience?" He turned his glance to Mary and asked quickly, "What is your name?"

"Mary Todd—Temple!" she said, flustered.

"Todd-Temple," the manager said, lifting his eyebrows. "An English name, I presume."

"Yes, yes," Mary stammered.

Mr Dumont murmured, "One moment, *s'il vous plaît*." He pressed a buzzer. The girls stood nervously. A moment later the door opened and a muscular, brawny man entered.

"You wanted somethin', boss?"

Mr Dumont drew the man aside and whispered.

"Got yuh, boss," the man said, then hurried outside.

The manager once more turned his attention to the girls. "So sorry. Now—if you will leave your names with me," he said, "I shall let you know. I have had several other applicants."

He handed a pad across the table and the girls wrote their names, addresses and phone numbers.

The three applicants thanked the restaurant manager and left his office. On the way through the restaurant, Callie, who was last, glimpsed three well-dressed men pushing open the swing doors to the kitchen. Their voices floated back and Callie caught a few words in a foreign tongue. "That's not French," she thought, surprised.

When the girls were outside, Mary whispered, "Oh, what an idiot I am for giving my real name."

"Don't worry," Callie said.

"Do you think Mr Dumont was suspicious of us at all?" Iola mused. "He kept looking at me funnily."

"It's just your imagination because we're playing detective," Callie said.

The girls were nearly at the jalopy when Pierre Dumont hastened from the restaurant towards them. Iola whirled. "He's after us. Run!"

·15·

A Growing Suspicion

THE frightened girls raced towards the car, but their speed was outmatched by Pierre Dumont. He overtook them halfway across the car-park.

"Wait!" he commanded. "Why are you running away?" He extended a handbag towards them.

"Oh dear," said Mary. "It's mine. I must have left it on your desk. Thank you."

"I return it with pleasure, mademoiselle," Dumont replied. With a slight bow, the manager walked away.

Callie sighed with relief, and the girls hastened towards Chet's car.

"Biff! We're here!" Iola said in a loud whisper.

No reply.

"What happened to our chauffeur?" Callie said, and opened the car door. She looked into the back seat and gasped.

Biff Hooper lay in a heap on the floor, with an ugly welt on the back of his head!

"Biff! What happened?" Iola cried. "Come on, girls. Let's lift him up." It took the combined strength of all three to lift big Biff onto the back seat.

"Thank goodness he's breathing!" declared Mary Todd, her hands trembling in fright.

While Callie chafed Biff's wrists, Iola patted his face gently until the youth opened his eyes.

"Ow, my head," Biff said, wincing. He touched the welt and winced again.

"Someone gave you an awful whack," said Iola. "Did you see who it was?"

"I didn't see anything but stars!" Biff commented wryly.

"There's something very odd going on around here," Iola, said with a determined set of her chin. "I'm going right back to talk with Mr Dumont."

"Wait a minute," Callie said, putting a restraining hand on Iola's arm. "If Dumont is in on all this, as I think he is, it won't do us any good. Let's report to Frank and Joe, quick."

"I think that would be better," Biff said. "Boy, am I groggy!"

"I'll drive back," Callie said. She hopped into the front seat while Mary and Iola remained in the back, on either side of Biff. Callie started the car, drove out of the car-park, and soon was whipping along the high-way towards Rockaway. She slowed down slightly for a right-hand curve. At the same instant a hedgehog plodded into the road. Desperately Callie swerved towards the centre of the road to avoid the creature. Just then another car sped towards them from the opposite direction.

Callie gripped the wheel and turned it hard. The cars passed with less than an inch to spare. With squealing brakes, both vehicles pulled over and stopped.

Frank, Joe and Chet hopped out of the Hardys' car and ran over to the girls and Biff.

"Whew!" said Joe. "That was a close call."

"I'm sorry," Callie said. "I—I didn't want to hit that poor animal."

"Forget it," said Joe. "What's the matter with you, Biff?"

"I'm all right now," the tall boy said, stepping out of the car with Iola and Mary. "Somebody conked me on the head. That's all."

"What!"

The girls told what had happened at the Palais Paris, and Mary said, "I don't trust that Pierre Dumont, in spite of his fancy French manners."

A quick comparison told the Hardys that the burly man to whom Dumont had whispered must have been Marcel.

"He might have been the one who hit you, Biff," Frank said. "Maybe Dumont ordered him to case the car and when he spotted you hiding in the back he let you have it."

When Callie told about the three men speaking in a foreign tongue, Frank and Joe exchanged meaningful glances.

"Good for you, Callie," Frank said. "But think hard, can't you identify the language?"

"No. I couldn't even guess," Callie replied.

"Let's go back and have a look-see," Joe said. "Besides, Frank, I brought along enough money to bail out your watch."

Chet transferred his gear, including the detector, to his jalopy, then took the wheel and followed the Hardys' car to the Palais Paris. By this time the car-park contained many cars.

"They must have really good food here," Iola commented.

"I hope it's better than their antiques," Joe said.

All three girls said they would like to see the antique shop.

"Okay," Joe said. "But don't try to buy anything. It'll fall apart!"

When the woman shopkeeper saw the Hardys she frowned, hastened into the back room, and reappeared with Marcel. Frank gave the girls a questioning glance. A nod from Iola told him it was indeed Marcel whom Dumont had summoned during their interview.

The muscular man did not bat an eyelid when he noticed Biff.

"Well," Marcel growled at the Hardys, "what do you want?"

"I came back to claim my watch," Frank said.

As Joe opened his wallet and took out the money, the woman reached under the counter.

"Thanks," Frank said, after the exchange was made. "Now all we have to do is put the spinning-wheel together."

Marcel smirked. "Tough luck."

"By the way," Joe said suddenly to the saleswoman, "where can we find Cadmus Quill?"

Her dark eyes darted to Marcel before she replied, "Cadmus Quill? I have never heard of him."

Marcel thrust his head forward menacingly and said, "All right. You got your watch, so scram out of here."

"But the girls want to look at your antiques," Frank persisted.

"Some other time," Marcel said, jerking his thumb

towards the door. "We don't want you kids in the way of the payin' customers."

Several patrons, having finished their luncheon, had wandered in and were looking about the shop.

"Okay," Frank said to the others. "Let's go."

When they reached the cars, Frank said, "Joe, I don't think you should have mentioned Quill."

"I thought I might catch them off guard," Joe replied.

"I think you did—trouble is, now they'll really be suspicious of us," Frank said, "provided Dad's report of Quill's connection here is correct."

"Where do we go from here?" Joe asked.

The young detectives held a hasty conference. "I suggest we pack up and go back to Bayport," Frank said. "Joe and I should talk with Dad and then decide on our next move."

The Hardys made a speedy trip to Rockaway for their gear and rejoined the others.

Biff rode in the Hardys' car with Frank and Joe, while Chet chauffeured the girls in his jalopy. Five miles later they stopped at the Hamburger Haven, piled out of the cars, and occupied counter stools.

After the girls had ordered, Chet boomed, "Three hamburgers for me, a double order of chips, and a thick chocolate malted drink."

While they chatted over their refreshing luncheon, the young detectives were amused by a small boy tumbling on a grassy plot outside the window. As Joe paid for the meal, the youngster ran up, crying.

"What's the matter?" Iola asked.

"I lost all my pennies," he said. "They dropped out of my pocket."

"Don't worry. We'll find them for you," Chet said importantly. He winked at Frank. "You see what I mean when I say that everybody should have a metal detector?"

"Okay, Sir Galahad," said Frank, "do your good deed for the day."

Chet hastened to his car. The others saw him frown. Then he ran to the Hardys' car and rummaged through it.

"What's the matter, Chet?" Biff called.

"My metal detector! It's gone!" Chet cried out in dismay.

·16·

Deadly Clicking

"YOUR detector *must* be in one of our cars," Joe said. "Come on. Let's look again."

But despite a thorough search of both vehicles, Chet's prized possession could not be found.

"There's only one answer," Chet said. "My metal detector was stolen while we were parked at the Palais Paris."

"You're telling me!" Biff put in. "That place is a jinx for us."

"I think Chet's right," Frank agreed. "Joe, you, Chet and I will go back to the restaurant. Biff can drive the girls to Bayport in the jalopy and take our gear too."

"Okay," Biff said. "But be careful of those monkeys at the Palais Paris. You know what one of 'em did to me."

Callie and Iola were reluctant to leave the Hardys, but conceded it was best that they return home with Biff.

"After all, we don't know how long the search will take," Iola said.

"Besides," Callie remarked with a twinkle, "I think we girl detectives have had enough excitement for one day!"

"Too much!" Mary declared.

After the girls and Biff were on their way, Frank, Joe and Chet hopped into the Hardys' car and drove directly to the Palais Paris.

Frank parked and the three boys entered the restaurant and walked briskly to the manager's office. They could see Dumont through the open door. He beckoned. "*Entrez*. Come in."

"We'd like to talk to you," Frank said seriously.

Dumont smiled. "No doubt you are seeking jobs," he said. "I am sorry to say that we do not have any—at present, that is. But you may give me your—"

"We don't want to work here!" Chet broke in tartly. "All I want is my metal detector. It was stolen from my car!"

"Metal detector? Ah, so that's what it is. You say stolen? *Ma foi!* Indeed, such is not the case."

Chet's eyes bulged as Dumont rose, walked to a small cupboard, and pulled out the missing detector.

"That's mine, all right," Chet said as the man handed the device over. "Where did *you* find it?"

"Precisely where you left it."

"It was left in the car," Frank said tersely. "Who swiped it? Do you know?"

A pained expression crossed Dumont's face. "It was not 'swiped,' as you Americans say," he retorted. "The detector was left standing in a corner of our antique shop."

Chet scratched his head and looked perplexed. "That's funny. I don't think I carried it in there—or did I?"

Now even the Hardys were stumped. Chet was so

fond of his new gadget he might conceivably have taken it inside. Frank gave their stout friend a questioning look. "Well, I can't remember taking it from the car, but I couldn't say for sure," Chet said. "Well, anyhow, thanks a lot, Mr Dumont," he added. "Mercy buckets, as you French say."

The manager rubbed a forefinger over his black moustache. "*Merci beaucoup*," he corrected, smiling. "Feel free to visit us any time."

The boys went outside and hurried towards their car. "He seemed like a nice enough guy," Chet remarked. "Compared to that Marcel character, anyhow."

Frank and Joe did not reply. Both were deep in thought about the strange incident. If Dumont had had the metal detector stolen, then why would he return it so graciously?

"As Shakespeare says, there's something rotten in Denmark, Joe," said Frank, as he slid behind the wheel.

"Denmark alias Palais Paris," Joe muttered.

Chet put his metal detector on the back seat, then sat in front between the Hardys. "Come on, Frank," he urged. "Let's see if we can catch up with my jalopy."

"Relax," Frank said. "I'm not going to break any speed limits."

"You can say that again," Joe replied. "We've had enough hard luck for one day."

The boys enjoyed the cool offshore breeze as they headed north towards Bayport along Shore Road. After ten miles, Frank stopped for a red light at an intersection. The engine purred quietly. All at once Joe's keen ears detected another sound.

Something was clicking on the back seat!

Joe jerked his head round. Nothing there but the metal detector. The boy reached back to turn it off. To his astonishment, the switch was already in "off" position.

"Frank!" Joe said tersely. "Quick! Pull over!"

The light had just shown green and Frank drove across the intersection and stopped on the shoulder of the road. "What—"

"Get out! Hurry!" Joe cried, opening his door and diving on to the ground. Frank did the same, and Chet followed a split second later.

Boom! A thunderous roar rent the air!

For a moment the Hardys lay half-stunned. Then Joe looked up. Smoke poured from the back of the car, which was a shambles. Frank raised his head and groaned at the sight. The brothers slowly got to their feet, but Chet remained face down in the dirt. The Hardys hastened to his side.

"Wh-what happened?" Chet asked in a weak voice, turning his head slightly.

"That detector of yours was booby-trapped," Joe said. He bent down to pick up the twisted metal, still warm from the blast.

Carefully Frank helped Chet get up. He swayed uncertainly, unable to regain his balance. "Everything's going in circles," he said. "Boy, I'm—I'm woozy!"

The Hardys sat him down beside the road, and flagged the first car that passed.

"Get help. We need the police and an ambulance!" Frank commanded.

"In a jiffy!" The driver sped off and the brothers placed Chet gently on a grassy spot beneath an oak tree.

"Jumpin' catfish!" Joe declared. "Our car's a wreck, Frank. What'll we do?"

"Have it towed back to Bayport for repairs. Hey, wait a minute!" Frank lifted the shattered boot lid. In the carton lay the pieces of spinning-wheel. These had not suffered any damage. Frank took out the carton.

Chet was very quiet. He merely stared at the sky until a siren sounded in the distance. First to appear on the scene was a state trooper car with two officers. It was followed by an ambulance, its red light blinking rapidly.

The brothers quickly identified themselves to the policemen, who recognized the Hardy name immediately. The officers gave their names as Starr and Dunn.

"What happened here?" Trooper Starr asked.

"An explosion," Frank said, pointing to the car. "Joe and I are okay, but our friend may be hurt."

Chet was lifted to a stretcher and placed in the ambulance. "We'll take him to Bayport Hospital," the driver said.

Frank and Joe tried to cheer their pal. "You'll be fine, Chet," said Joe. "Just relax and obey the doctor's orders."

"We'll see you soon," Frank added.

Chet attempted a grin. "You sleuths will have to get along without me, I guess."

The ambulance doors were closed, and with siren wailing, it sped north along the highway.

Trooper Dunn then radioed for a vehicle to tow the damaged car to a repair shop in Bayport. "It won't be here for another hour," Dunn told the boys. "No use your waiting. We'll take you home after we hear your story."

Frank and Joe briefed the troopers about the strange disappearance of the metal detector at the Palais Paris and the officers promised to make an investigation. They took the detector as evidence. Then, at top speed, Trooper Starr drove the boys—and their spinning-wheel—to their front door.

Mr Hardy himself came out and shook hands with the officers, old friends of his. After Starr and Dunn had driven off, the detective and his sons went into the living-room. Frank took the wooden pieces from the carton and put them on the floor.

"Dad, we've had a terrible time," Joe began.

"I know something about it," Mr Hardy said. "Mr Morton phoned me. You'll be glad to know that Chet is suffering only from shock and has been taken home."

"Thank goodness!" Frank said.

"Now come up to my study and we'll go over the whole situation," Mr Hardy said.

Mrs Hardy brought glasses of lemonade, and the three sleuths discussed every angle of the Todd-Quill case, while sipping the cool beverage.

"I'm convinced the Palais Paris is involved in some way," Frank concluded.

"It would seem so," Fenton Hardy agreed. "Tell me more about this Commander Wilson."

The boys took turns at relating their weird experiences at the Honeycomb Caves.

"E. K. T. Wilson's just plain loony," Joe stated flatly.

"I wouldn't agree with you one hundred per cent,"

his father said. "If Wilson is as insane as he seems, I think he would be in an institution."

"You mean maybe he's not crazy at all?" asked Frank. "It's an act?"

Their father thought that this was a possibility, however remote, and advised his sons to pursue the Wilson angle with all their power.

"I'll tell you why, boys. Your enemies are on the run!"

"You really think so?" Joe asked.

"Absolutely. They're desperate. The booby-trapped detector proves it. When they find that you three escaped, the criminals will show their hand again. Mark my words. So be extra careful."

Fenton Hardy went on to say there were no new developments in the radar station case. "Things have been quiet," he said. "Too quiet."

"Like the calm before the storm," Joe said.

Just then the Hardys' doorbell chimed. The boys heard their mother answer it and exclaim, "Gertrude Hardy! I'm so glad to see you!"

Frank and Joe exchanged wry grins. "Speaking of storms," said Frank, "Aunt Gertrude has arrived."

The detectives broke off their conference and went down to greet the visitor. Gertrude Hardy was a tall, angular woman with a strong personality. She was most emphatically not in favour of her nephews following in the footsteps of her famous brother.

"Chasing criminals is no pastime for young boys" was one of her favourite expressions. But beneath her peppery manner, Aunt Gertrude held a warm affection for Frank and Joe, and they for her.

"Hi, Aunt Gertrude!" Joe said.

"Good to see you again," said Frank.

Without any ado whatsoever, Aunt Gertrude pulled a hatpin from her bun, removed her flowered hat, set it on the sofa, and demanded, "Where's my spinning-wheel?"

"Why—why—Aunt Gertrude—" Joe began.

"Don't stall," Miss Hardy said sternly. "Your mother just told me that you purchased a spinning-wheel."

"We did," Frank said.

"Well, where is it?"

Joe feebly pointed to the spindles and other accessories lying on the floor.

"That? That's my spinning-wheel?" Aunt Gertrude gasped.

· 17 ·

A Bold Warning

WITH the withering directness of a district attorney, Aunt Gertrude questioned her nephews about the broken spinning-wheel. Mr and Mrs Hardy did a magnificent job of suppressing smiles as their relative relentlessly pursued her cross-examination.

"You say you broke it, Joe? How?"

"It was hanging from the ceiling and I touched it."

"Now, Joe, refresh your memory!" Aunt Gertrude said. "A spinning-wheel on the ceiling! Bosh!"

Frank sprang to his brother's defence. "But it was only on display," he explained. "It wasn't for sale."

"Sakes alive! Then why did you buy it?" Aunt Gertrude said.

"We had to," Joe said. "There was this big husky fellow, Marcel—"

Aunt Gertrude threw up her hands. "What imaginations!" she exclaimed.

"It's the truth, every word of it," Frank insisted. "We can prove—"

"Oh, I believe you." Aunt Gertrude tossed her head vigorously. "Although the whole thing is beyond me!" Without another word, Miss Hardy scooped up the pile and marched from the room into the kitchen. In a moment her footsteps could be heard descending to the basement.

Frank and Joe looked at their parents and shrugged in embarrassment.

"Don't worry," Mrs Hardy smiled. "Your Aunt Gertrude really appreciates what you boys have done."

A telephone call to the Morton home that evening revealed Chet was progressing nicely. "His hair was singed a little at the back," Mrs Morton told Frank. "But otherwise he's pretty much recovered from the shock. Why don't you and Joe come over and see him tomorrow morning?"

"Fine. We will."

Before going to bed, the brothers went to the kitchen for a snack. Aunt Gertrude was there. Still embarrassed about the spinning-wheel, Frank and Joe grinned sheepishly. But their aunt seemed to be in good spirits and handed them her personal cheque for fifty dollars in payment for the antique.

"Junipers!" Joe said. "That's swell of you, considering the condition it's in."

Thoroughly rested after a good night's sleep, the brothers had breakfast and got ready to visit their stout friend. Frank took a few moments to call Biff. "Sorry I can't join you fellows today," Biff said. "Too much work around the house. But in case of an emergency don't hesitate to holler. And tell Chet to keep his chins up."

Mr Hardy had given his sons permission to use his car, but as they were about to step out of the back door, their mother stopped them. "Aren't you taking Chet some flowers?"

"Flowers?" Joe said. "Oh, Mom, of course not."

"Well, you should take the patient something," Mrs Hardy persisted.

"You're right. How about a fruit basket?" Frank suggested.

Their mother nodded approvingly. "A good idea—cater to Chet's appetite."

"He takes pretty good care of that himself," Joe said. "All right, we'll stop at the store on our way."

The boys drove to the heart of Bayport, where they stopped at a fancy food shop. There the proprietor made up an attractive basket of fruit, covered with transparent plastic and topped by bright red ribbon.

As they drove out of town over the country road to the Morton farmhouse, Frank and Joe discussed their next step in solving the mystery of the missing Morgan Todd.

"Dad thinks we should investigate Commander Wilson further, so we'll do it," said Frank. "Remember Todd's riddle of the word *Rockaway*. We still have more sleuthing to do around Honeycomb Caves."

"When do we start?" Joe asked impatiently.

"As soon as we visit Chet." Frank turned off the road into the driveway of the Morton home and parked. Between them, the Hardys carried the large fruit basket into the house. They were met at the front door by Mary Todd.

"Oh, how gorgeous!" she said, admiring the colourful gift.

Mrs Morton came downstairs and greeted the boys warmly. "I think Chet can see you now," she said, adding that Iola was out shopping.

Mary and the brothers mounted the stairs to the second floor. "I hope he's feeling very much better," Frank said.

"He's quite comfortable," Mary said. "That poor, brave boy!"

When they entered Chet's room, Frank and Joe looked about, amazed. His bed was flanked by two bouquets of flowers. On the bedside table lay a half empty box of chocolates and a quart bottle of raspberry squash, four-fifths consumed.

Reclining on three fluffed pillows lay Chet, with a cherubic look on his round face.

"Hi, fellows," he said feebly with a wave of his hand. "How's tricks?"

"Jumpin' catfish!" Joe exclaimed. "You got the best trick of all. How about it, Frank, let's get ourselves blasted too?"

"It isn't any fun," Chet said, and with a look of pain held his hand to his forehead.

Instantly Mary Todd sprang to his side with a cool, damp cloth which she placed over his brow. "You poor dear," she said, and Joe gulped.

Frank stifled a grin. "We're going back to the caves," he announced. Chet's reaction was startling. He whipped off the compress and sat up.

"You are? Take me along, will you? That fishing was great!"

"We're not going fishing—not for fish, that is," Frank said.

"More sleuthing? Ugh!" Chet groaned and sank back on the pillows.

"Well, now that you're a celebrity," Joe said teasingly, "enjoy it while you can, Chet, old boy."

This seemed to revive the chubby patient. "May I have another drink of squash, Mary?" he asked. His young nurse nimbly moved to the other side of the bed and poured a glass of the sparkling beverage. Chet drank it and lay back again. "Yes, I guess I am a celebrity, fellows. The reporter got my personal story this morning."

"Reporter?" Frank said quickly.

"Yes," Mary put in, "from the *Bayport Times*."

"Mary made a big hit with him," Chet went on with a grin. "He asked a lot of questions about her, too."

"Wait a minute," Joe said. "What was this fellow's name?"

"Otto Lippincott." Mary supplied the answer.

"I never heard of anyone by that name on the *Times*," Frank said.

Frank excused himself to make a phone call and hurried downstairs. He returned ten minutes later, his face flushed with excitement.

"There is no Lippincott who works for that newspaper," he said. "Chet, you've been duped."

Disappointment, then indignation, crossed Chet's face. "Do you mean that guy was a phoney?" he blurted.

"Nothing else but. He came here to fish for information," Frank replied.

Joe turned to Mary and asked, "How much did you tell this man?"

"Oh, have I done the wrong thing again?" Mary wailed.

"Well, maybe," Frank declared. "But it's too late to worry over spilled milk. From now on I advise both of you to keep mum on anything you know."

Just then the front door slammed and Iola's cheerful voice floated up the stairs. "Frank, Joe. Are you here?"

Joe blushed a little. "Yes, Iola, come on up."

Quick footsteps sounded on the stairs and Iola hurried into Chet's room. In her hand she held a white envelope. "I found this in the mailbox," she said. "No stamp or anything. It just says 'Chet Morton.' "

"Another well-wisher, I suppose," Chet said importantly, and took the envelope. He tore off one end, blew into the slit, and removed the note.

"Good grief! Listen!" He read, " *Get Hardys off case or your life will be in danger.* "

Iola gasped and clutched Mary's hand. "Oh, this is terrible!" she cried out.

Frank frowned and bit his lip. "I didn't want to get your family involved, Chet."

"What'll we do?" Joe asked.

Frank's mind worked rapidly. "We'll get Sam Radley to stand constant guard on the house here," he said. "After dark tonight we'll smuggle Mary to our house. Mother and Aunt Gertrude can stand watch over her there."

"I'll say!" Chet said. "I wouldn't want to be the one to cross your Aunt Gertrude's path."

A telephone call to the Hardy home confirmed Frank's protection plan, and Sam Radley, who fortunately was in town, told the boys he would report to the Morton farm.

When Mr Hardy's operator arrived about noon, Frank and Joe excused themselves and returned home.

Frank telephoned Bayport Police Headquarters and notified Chief Collig about the impostor and the threat Chet received. Collig promised to dispatch a squad car to patrol the area during the night and relieve Radley.

"What about Honeycomb Caves?" Joe asked, after his brother had finished the call.

"We'll tackle them tonight," Frank said. "As soon as we have Mary safely here."

"Shall we go in the *Sleuth*?"

Frank mulled over the question. Finally he shook his head. "Going by water is a good idea, Joe, but these crooks are keeping close tabs on us and would probably recognize our boat."

"How about using Biff's?" Joe suggested. "He says the *Envoy* just got a new engine and it's in great shape."

Frank phoned Biff immediately and arranged to use his speedboat for the brothers' sleuthing adventure.

The Hardys thanked their pal, who kept his craft in a boathouse half a mile from the Hardys'. After supper Frank and Joe packed their gear to have it in readiness. Then they drove out to Chet's place.

"Is Mary ready to come with us?" Joe asked Iola, as they stepped into the hall.

"Just about."

The Hardys heard footsteps on the stairs and glanced up to see a slim, handsome young man descending. He wore dungarees, work jacket and farm hat.

"Hey!" Frank cried out. "That's not a guy, that's a gal!"

Mary Todd grinned in her disguise. "Iola and I thought up the idea. Like it?"

"Terrific." Joe nodded approval. "You two have the true detective spirit."

Chet, who appeared fully recovered, now came downstairs.

"I thought you were still shell-shocked," said Joe, with a sly look at their stout friend.

"Without a nurse I'm better already," quipped Chet. Then he took on a serious demeanour. "Now look, fellows, be extra careful of Mary, won't you?"

With a promise that they would, the Hardys left the Morton house and drove Mary to their own home.

Aunt Gertrude and Mrs Hardy received the girl kindly, and showed her to the second guest room.

Biff Hooper arrived minutes later and drove the brothers to his dock. In a few minutes the two sleuths and their gear were aboard the *Envoy*. Joe started the engine.

"I checked the running lights," Biff said. "Everything is okay."

The Hardys thanked him and shoved off, with Joe at the wheel. The *Envoy* knifed through the waters of Barmet Bay, its shore front twinkling with lights. As the boys passed the boathouse where the *Sleuth* was kept, Frank called out, "Throttle down, Joe. What's that light over there?"

Joe brought the *Envoy* about and saw a light flickering from the window of their boathouse. "Jeepers! I don't know!" He extinguished the running lights and crept quietly over the dark waters.

As they neared the boathouse Frank suddenly exclaimed in alarm. Smoke was seeping out from beneath the door. Their boathouse was on fire!

· 18 ·

Searchlight

THE wailing of a police siren drifted across Barmet Bay, followed by the clanging bells of a fire engine. Now the window glass of the Hardy boathouse broke with the heat, and flames licked out, illuminating the water.

With one hand on the steering wheel, Joe reached over for the fire extinguisher clamped on the side of the *Envoy*. Throttle open, the craft leaped through the water until Frank called out:

"Joe! Slow down."

"Why? Our whole boathouse will burn up."

"The fire department will take care of it." Frank had hardly spoken before an arch of water was sprayed against the building and the flames were being quenched.

As Joe slackened speed and circled about, Frank explained, "This blaze could have been set for two reasons. One, to keep us from using the *Sleuth*, and two—"

"I get you already," Joe said. "A diversionary action!"

"Exactly." Frank nodded. "If our enemies are up to

something tonight, they'll want to pin us down in Bayport."

By now the smoke too had abated, and firemen raised the door of the boathouse. In the glow of their lanterns, the brothers could see that the *Sleuth* was still afloat.

"She may not be badly damaged," Frank said. "At any rate, we can't stop to see now. On to Honeycomb Caves, Joe."

Unfortunately, the *Envoy* did not have a ship-to-shore radio, as did the *Sleuth*. The brothers therefore could not communicate with their home, but knew that Mr Hardy would be notified of the boathouse fire soon enough.

Joe snapped on the running lights again, and the *Envoy* purred through the rolling waves as its pilot guided the craft expertly along the coast he knew so well.

After the *Envoy* passed a blinking buoy marking the entrance to Barmet Bay, the run south was nearly a straight line. But even with smooth sailing, it was nearly two a.m. before the great cliffs loomed in shadowy silhouettes on their starboard side.

Joe throttled back, and the *Envoy* rocked in the waves as the young detectives discussed their next move.

"Let's cruise past the caves as close as we can get," Frank said. "After that, we can put in at John Donachie's dock."

Frank took turns with his brother at the wheel, and, guiding the *Envoy* silently towards shore, the boys studied the Honeycomb Caves. The half-moon illuminated the shore just enough to make the dark cave openings look like the baleful eye sockets of a skull.

The craft ran parallel to the shore, and as they neared Commander Wilson's cave house, Joe chuckled. "I'll bet the old boy is sawing wood right now— For Pete's sake, Frank!"

The brothers were startled by a brilliant finger of light which suddenly shot from the cave mouth across the water.

"A giant searchlight!" declared Frank.

The bow of the *Envoy* nearly touched the edge of the powerful beam, and Frank turned hard on the wheel to reverse his course. The light moved away from the boat, giving its churning wake a chance to settle in the darkness unseen. Frank and Joe bent low, hoping the wave troughs would conceal the *Envoy*. Then the light disappeared as suddenly as it had swept the green sea.

"Junipers!" said Joe. "That was a close squeak!"

"Came right from Wilson's cave!" Frank exclaimed. "Dad hit it on the nose. Wilson's not nutty at all. He's as sane as we are, and up to something sinister."

"Do you suppose he picked us up on radar, or heard our engine?" Joe pondered as Frank made a big circle and headed for the fisherman's dock.

"It might have been a signal," Frank said. "And we just happened on it by luck."

"A signal for what," Joe asked, "or to what?"

"Maybe a ship lying offshore, or men waiting in a small boat. Who knows?"

"How can we find out?"

Frank replied with determination, "Maybe Johnny Donachie can help us. If he'll take us fishing with him tomorrow, we can lie low offshore and spy on the caves with binoculars."

"Great idea," Joe said approvingly. "Too bad we'll wake him up in the middle of the night."

When the *Envoy* docked at Johnny's pier, Frank and Joe got their first good look at the fisherman's craft. It was a little more than thirty feet in length, with a cabin sticking up like an inverted cheese box.

"A pretty old tub," said Joe, as he hopped out of the *Envoy* and made fast.

"Looks sort of top-heavy," Frank said. "But if it suits Johnny Donachie, it's okay with me."

The brothers walked up to the dark house. Frank took a deep breath and knocked on the door. Seconds later a yellow light blinked on and a sleepy voice sounded behind the closed door. "Who's there?"

"Frank and Joe Hardy."

The door opened a crack and the fisherman looked out.

"Thunderation!" he said, opening the door to admit the boys. "What brings you out at this hour?"

"We're doing some more detective work," Joe replied. "Did you see the light down the coast tonight?"

The fisherman said that he had noticed a glow in the night sky several times. "It's weird. That's why I stay away from that spooky place."

"We have a favour to ask," Frank said. "Will you take us fishing tomorrow?"

"Sure, don't see why not. Hey, you boys must be tired. We have an extra room."

"Thanks, but we can sleep in our boat," said Frank.

By this time Mrs Donachie had been awakened and insisted that the Hardys stay for the rest of the night.

Secretly Frank and Joe were glad to accept and slept soundly until they were aroused for breakfast.

After they had eaten, the boys covered the *Envoy* with a tarpaulin, then joined Johnny on his boat, which bore the faded name *Lena*. The fisherman started the noisy engine, and with a *clink-clunk-clink-clunk* the old craft limped seaward.

At Frank's request, Johnny headed down the coast parallel to the caves but far enough out to avoid suspicion. Frank and Joe crouched behind the gunwales, keeping their binoculars trained on shore.

Half an hour elapsed. Suddenly Joe straightened. "I see some people!" he said.

"Me too. And look. Isn't that Wilson up there?"

"Moving around like an athlete!" Joe observed.

The commander and three other men were carrying boxes into the cave mouth.

The boys' arms ached from their steady surveillance. At last, two hours later, Wilson reappeared. He sat in front of his cave for a while, then moved off to the cavern in which the Hardys had stayed and appeared to examine it briefly before returning to his own headquarters.

"Frank, we have to get ashore and find out what's going on," Joe said.

"That may come sooner than we expect," his brother replied, glancing up into the lowering sky.

The waves became a deeper green and the lacy tops were flicked off by the freshening breeze.

"Fishin's over for the day," Johnny told the boys. "We got to go back."

"How about a little longer look," Joe coaxed, seeing Wilson stride along the shore.

"These storms come up awful fast," Johnny said. "We'd best be puttin' back." But the Hardys finally coaxed the fisherman to remain for a short while in order to spy on Wilson. Almost immediately, the fishing boat began to lurch as the waves grew higher.

"Can't stay another second," Johnny said. "It's gettin' dangerous."

With a *clink-clunk* the old motor-powered *Lena* chugged slowly back towards the fisherman's wharf.

"Can't you give her more speed, Johnny?" Joe called out as the waves grew taller and the wind whistled about their ears.

"Six knots is the best she can do."

They were halfway to their destination when a huge wave crashed upon the deck, nearly washing Joe into the sea. But the boy clung to a railing post until Frank dragged him into the safety of the cabin.

The old tub now listed badly. "We'll never make it!" Johnny said gloomily, as the rough sea bullied the boat about and rain lashed the waves.

Just then Joe looked towards shore and exclaimed, "Frank! Is that the *Envoy* I see?"

Frank raised his binoculars. "It sure is. Well, what do you know? Johnny, your wife's coming to our rescue."

Minutes later, Mrs Donachie came about in the *Envoy*. Joe threw a line to her and, with the sea heaving about them, the woman towed *Lena* to shore. When both craft had been moored at the dock, they hastened inside the house, soaking wet.

Frank shook his head. "I've got to hand it to you, Mrs Donachie. You certainly have a lot of courage."

"And skill too," Joe said admiringly.

The woman pushed back wisps of damp hair and replied with a smile, "What do you expect from a fisherman's wife?"

By early evening the rain had ceased and the skies were clear. After a hearty supper John Donachie pushed his chair back from the table, lighted his pipe, then said, "Now that the storm's over, are you boys takin' the *Envoy* back to Bayport?"

Joe shook his head. "Frank and I want to get closer to those caves and see what's going on."

"At night?" The Donachies looked fearful.

"Yes. As soon as it gets dark enough," Frank said.

"We should be back before daybreak," Joe added, testing his flashlight.

After many admonitions to be careful, the boys disappeared along the trail in the darkness. The climb to the top of the cliffs was arduous, but the way was clear in the moonlight.

"Here's the ravine," Joe said finally, and the brothers made their way down to the sandy beach. There they stopped for a moment to get their bearings.

"We'll have to crouch low and stay as close to the cliff as possible," Frank advised. "I'll lead the way."

The Hardys passed the mouth of their old cave and crept stealthily towards Wilson's cavern. Suddenly Frank pulled Joe back into a crevice of rock. "Good grief!" he whispered. "Look out there!"

Three hundred yards offshore a small red light winked like the eye of a sea monster. But even in the gloom the boys recognized a conning tower.

"A submarine!" Joe exclaimed.

· 19 ·

A Raft of Trouble

THE magnitude of the mystery they had uncovered hit Frank and Joe like a stunning blow. This was it! Commander Wilson was a fraud, a cover-up for some sort of gang receiving supplies and men by secret submarine at the Honeycomb Caves.

Another light winked from in front of Wilson's cave. Slowly the sub surfaced, its whaleback silhouette standing out in the darkness.

"They've contacted each other," said Joe. "If we only had a boat."

"I have an idea," Frank said. "We'll swim out to the sub." He stripped down to his shorts and Joe did the same. "We might make it if Wilson doesn't turn on the big searchlight."

The brothers concealed their clothes behind a rock, then waded into the surf. They dived into a wave and, with strong overhand strokes, rapidly swam towards the submarine. Silently the Hardys came up to the undersea craft, and treading water, clung to the hull.

Tensely the boys waited. A few moments later the hatch opened. Frank and Joe held their breaths as six men piled out, dragging a large rubber life raft. They flung it into the water with a *plop*, and stepped inside, where two of their number manned paddles.

Hearts thumping wildly, Frank and Joe pressed back against the sub, their faces barely showing above water, ten feet away from the raft.

The men spoke a strange foreign language, but suddenly one said sternly in English, "Do not use the mother tongue. It is dangerous. We are now in America!"

Frank decided on a bold strategy, and nudged his brother. "Come on!"

Swiftly the boys pushed off and swam underwater to emerge silently right behind the raft. They reached up and gripped it with one hand, scissor-kicking so as not to be a drag on the rubber craft as the paddlers guided it across the waves towards shore.

The brothers glanced back, to see the conning tower of the sub disappear beneath the waves.

"Ah, there's Wilson's light!" came a voice from the raft.

"Yes, our calculations were correct," said another man. "We will show these Americans!"

Finally Frank and Joe felt their toes touch bottom. When the men hopped out, the boys swam underwater away from shore, then surfaced and once more trod water. This time their eyes fell upon a most unusual scene. In the glow of the light inside Wilson's cave, they saw the commander greet each of the new arrivals, pumping their hands as they stepped inside.

But there was something different about Wilson. His

face looked younger. And . . . his hair was now black.

"Wilson's no old man. That was a grey wig he was wearing!" hissed Joe. "He used face make-up too."

"There's no time to lose!" Frank said, and both boys swam to the beach. The only evidence of activity was the dim glow coming from the cave mouth. Now and then it faded as if those inside were milling about.

The Hardys quickly got their clothes and slipped them on. "If we only had some help," Frank said, as they inched closer to the entrance of the cave. From within came the hum of voices.

They halted and looked about in the darkness. "I think they would have posted a sentry," Frank said. "Do you see anybody, Joe?"

Joe flashed his light up and down the beach, but could see no one. "What now, Frank?"

"Into the cave. We've got to see what this is all about."

The brothers listened, but the voices had receded. Only muffled sounds emerged from the cavern. Clutching their flashlights, Frank and Joe slipped inside. At first the interior looked much the same as the first time they had seen it. The shotgun lay on the ledge, the code book was still in evidence, and the food supply was stashed as it had been previously.

But as the boys penetrated deeper, their mouths fell open in wonderment. To the rear of the cave was a thick electrical conduit which snaked back into the cavern. Tiptoeing forward, Frank and Joe finally came to a thick wooden partition with an iron door.

"Good grief!" Joe declared. "Frank, this is set up like a hidden city."

"I think those men might be spies, or saboteurs," Frank whispered. "Maybe they're connected with the trouble at the radar site."

"But what about Quill and Todd?" Joe asked. "How do they fit into all this?"

"I don't know yet. But we've found the mine that Chet discovered," Frank said. "That metal conduit. And it makes a beeline to the Palais Paris."

"I could just smell something phoney about that whole place," Joe declared, moving closer to the iron door. "Frank, let's go in!"

"Okay, I'm game. But we'd better stick close together."

Joe's hand reached for the door handle. Suddenly a voice behind them froze the boys into immobility.

"Hardys, you're through!"

The boys wheeled about. Joe gasped. "Cadmus Quill!"

The short, bouncy college instructor leered at them. Behind him stood four henchmen.

"You're trapped!" Cadmus Quill said.

Frank whispered to his brother and Joe nodded. As Quill and his strong-arm men advanced, the boys uttered a bloodcurling war-cry and charged like half-backs! Joe tackled two of the men, bowling them over. They scrambled to their feet and grabbed Joe. He twisted frantically to escape their grip. Frank doubled Quill with a blow to the solar plexus, then dashed past the other two men towards the cave mouth. They darted after him.

Frank's plan was working! With speed born of desperation, the boy leaped towards the ledge and grabbed the shotgun. Then he aimed it overhead, close to the electrical conduit.

Frank pulled the trigger. There was a deafening blast and a shower of sparks. The lights went out and an acrid pall of smoke filled the cavern.

·20·

Loyal Pals

THE sudden blast and blackout threw the Hardys' assailants into confusion. The next moment, youthful shouts were heard from the entrance, and two flashlights illuminated the cave.

"Frank! Joe! What's going on?" came Chet's voice.

"Wow! They need help!" cried Biff.

Quill and his four thugs, seeing the reinforcements, dashed to the iron door and jerked it open. The four young sleuths raced after them, but were too late. The fugitives disappeared inside, the door clanged shut, and a bolt clicked fast. The brothers, then Biff and Chet, tried the handle to no avail.

"How did you know we were here?" Frank asked.

"Chet and I got to thinking about you two working on this case all alone," Biff said. "So we drove down to Johnny Donachie's. We missed you by minutes."

"So we climbed up the cliffs and down the ravine," Chet added.

"And made it here just in time," Joe said. "I don't think we could have scared them off much longer without you."

"That isn't all," Biff went on. He said that before they had left Bayport, Mr Hardy had alerted the State

Police to search the Palais Paris. "Some of the cops are on their way to the caves too."

The boys heard scuffling sounds coming from behind the iron door.

"Sounds like somebody running," Joe said.

"And stumbling about in the dark," Frank added.

The brothers reasoned that the short-circuited conduit had also blacked out the area beyond Wilson's cave.

Just then the rumpus inside was accompanied by frantic shouts. The bolt clicked, and as it did, Frank and Joe grabbed the handle and held it tightly.

"We've got them trapped, and we're going to keep them that way!" Frank declared.

The melee within grew in intensity. It was punctuated by a shot. Someone groaned. Then came banging on the iron door.

"Frank and Joe, if that's you, open up!"

"Dad!" Joe exclaimed, hardly daring to believe his ears.

"Open up, boys. We've caught the gang."

The brothers let go the handle and stepped back as the door swung inward. Several great searchlights illuminated the chamber and Fenton Hardy stepped out. He was followed by six policemen, each of whom had a manacled prisoner in tow. One of the prisoners the boys recognized as E. K. T. Wilson. He glowered at them balefully.

"Great going, Dad!" Frank exclaimed. He now reported the submarine incident and had just finished when two state troopers dashed in through the beach entrance. They were officers Starr and Dunn. "Have you got them all rounded up?" Trooper Dunn asked.

"I think so," Fenton Hardy replied. "But there's one man still missing—Morgan Todd. We think he's around here somewhere."

Upon learning of the sub, Trooper Starr switched on his portable radio transmitter and broadcast an urgent request to intercept the undersea prowler.

Revelations came so thick and fast that Frank and Joe were dazed by the hornets' nest which they had uncovered. At Fenton Hardy's direction, the troopers took up positions at the mouth of the cave while the rest of the party pressed deeper into the passageway behind the iron door.

The gradient was up, and as the boys marched along they could see that the tunnel was man-made. The walls and ceiling bore the marks of excavating tools, and here and there the passage was shored with planks.

Finally Fenton Hardy led the young sleuths to a flight of concrete steps. They ascended to a metal door, opened it, and found themselves in the kitchen of the Palais Paris!

There, on the floor and manacled back to back, sat Dumont and Marcel. They glared at the Hardys with hate-filled eyes.

"They're the ones who did this to us!" Marcel said bitterly. "If they hadn't come snooping—"

"Shut up!" Dumont snapped. "Fool!"

"It's okay for you, big shot," Marcel complained. "You've got plenty of dough to help you. But not me!"

Police Chief Collig of Bayport and two of his men stood by with drawn pistols as three other gang members were flushed from upstairs rooms at the Palais Paris.

"I think we have them all rounded up now, Fenton," Collig said.

"Good work. The Federal men will be here any minute."

A sound of sirens from a distance reached their ears. They howled like banshees as they drew closer, then petered out in front of the Palais Paris. Car doors banged shut, and ten Federal agents burst into the restaurant.

Dumont and Marcel were pulled to their feet, and stood in line with the rest of the prisoners as the government men entered the kitchen.

"You've done a splendid job for us, Fenton," said a tall man with hair greying at the temples.

Mr Hardy turned to his sons. "This is Special Agent Alberts," he said, and made the introductions. Then the detective added, "Actually, my sons and their friends cracked this case. My credit is secondary."

"Well, you all did a magnificent job," Alberts told the four boys.

"But we still haven't solved the mystery of the missing Morgan Todd," Frank said.

"You found Morgan Todd all right," Agent Alberts said, grinning at the young detectives.

"*What?*" they chorused.

The tale which the Federal men unfolded nearly defied imagination. The Hardys' warning about the sub had been relayed instantly to the Navy, and Coast Guard. Destroyer depth charges in the area off the caves had forced the craft to the surface.

"The Navy has caught a nice prize," Alberts said. "And your friend Todd, who'd been imprisoned on the sub, is aboard one of our destroyers this moment, safe and sound."

Hearing this, Joe dashed to the telephone and called the Hardy home. He spoke to his mother, who relayed the good news to Mary. He could hear Mary's cry of delight, and then sobbing, as she broke down and wept with joy.

A police van carried the prisoners to Bayport for further interrogation. Biff Hooper went back in the *Envoy*, while the Hardys, Chet and Agent Alberts returned in a police car. It was then the boys learned the true magnitude of their case.

"Morgan Todd was the key to the whole mystery," Mr Hardy told them. The young instructor had, while abroad, stumbled upon bizarre information. The foreign country in which he was studying had set up a spy and saboteur centre in the Honeycomb Caves. Also, they had engineers working on a project designed to nullify the effect of the new U.S. Coastal Radar Station at Telescope Hill.

"A device was to be raised out of the cave area at night," Agent Alberts said, "that would have jammed the radar signals."

"But where does the Palais Paris come in?" asked Frank.

"That was a front," Mr Hardy said. "The gang's engineers constructed the tunnel to lead directly from the Palais Paris to the shore, and enlarge the caves."

"And credit for that discovery goes to Chet," Frank

said, slapping the stout boy on the shoulder. "His metal detector did the trick!"

"And the U.S. Government," the Federal agent said, "is going to reimburse you, Chet, for your detector, and also for repairs to your car, Frank and Joe."

Alberts went on to explain that Morgan Todd, being cautious and conservative, had decided to conduct a solo investigation of the caves before turning over his information to the U.S. Government.

"I'll bet that's where he made a mistake," Chet commented.

"Right. Cadmus Quill, who had been brainwashed by the foreign spy ring into being a traitor, helped to kidnap Todd. But before they carried him away that night, Todd begged them to allow him to prepare the examination for his students."

"A pretty clever fellow," Mr Hardy conceded, "to leave that Rockaway tip. And you boys did a grand job in discovering it."

"Commander Wilson had me fooled," Joe said wryly, as the car neared Bayport.

"Dad had the right angle on him," Frank said.

When the limousine pulled up in front of the Hardy house, Alberts said he would drive Chet home. They would all meet Chief Collig for a conference at Bayport Police Headquarters at ten o'clock the next morning.

It was nearly daylight when Frank and Joe fell asleep. They awakened later to learn that all of Bayport was buzzing with the excitement of the great coup the boys had pulled off.

Frank and Joe went to headquarters with Mary Todd. In Chief Collig's office they were joined by

Chet, Biff, Iola and Callie. Then two Federal agents appeared with Morgan Todd. He and his sister flung themselves into each other's arms in a fond embrace.

Morgan Todd shook hands vigorously with the Hardys. "I can't thank you enough for saving my life!" he said warmly. Todd revealed that the submarine was to have taken him to a remote part of the world, where he would have been incarcerated for the rest of his life.

"We have some other interesting details too," Alberts said. "Commander E. K. T. Wilson was a phoney, of course. In his younger days he was an actor, who defected while in the service of his country on a foreign tour of duty."

"That nutty bit of his nearly paid off," said Joe, "with that shooting and all."

Frank grinned. "Good thing he overdid it somewhat, at least enough for Dad to catch on."

Chief Collig reported that Wilson, under relentless quizzing, had admitted losing the pistol on the beach the night he had prowled about the boys' cave. As for the stacked wood, it had been left there by picnickers months before. An expert on explosives, Wilson had been called by Dumont to booby-trap the metal detector.

When Iola Morton asked if there would be any international complications as a result of the Hardys' victory, the agent said, "The State Department has already successfully negotiated the matter."

It was also revealed that Pierre Dumont, the spies' chief man in the U.S., came from a French-speaking part of the world and had applied for U.S. citizenship.

Marcel had worked under him abroad and was merely a strong-arm dupe. The woman shopkeeper at the Palais Paris was found to be innocent of any wrongdoing.

"And what about the foreign caps?" Joe asked.

"A careless mistake on the saboteurs' part," Fenton Hardy answered.

The boys learned that the henchman who had dropped his cap at the radar site had also posed later as the newspaper reporter. The same foreigner also had set the boathouse on fire.

Mr Hardy smiled proudly. "You boys were really on the ball!"

"And I'd say that the U.S. Government is in debt to all of you who worked on this case," Agent Alberts added.

The *Bayport Times* had already bannerlined the Hardys' feat, and the telephone rang with congratulatory messages all day.

That evening Mrs Hardy was hostess at a get-together in the detectives' home. Happy, excited voices filled the living-room as Laura Hardy and Aunt Gertrude served refreshments. In the midst of the gaiety a telegram was received by the Hardy boys. It came from Kenworthy College and stated that the fraternity had expelled Cadmus Quill. The message also contained an apology to the Hardys, and congratulations on their patriotic efforts.

Then Joe turned on the record-player. Chet, usually bashful with girls, asked Mary Todd to dance, and soon the living-room was a blur of motion as the young people gyrated to the latest steps.

"I guess your brother wasn't planning to get married after all," Chet said.

"What!"

"Oh, nothing. Just another one of Quill's lies."

When the music was over, Mrs Hardy smilingly called for attention. The young folks gathered in a circle, and Aunt Gertrude emerged majestically from the kitchen, carrying a spinning-wheel.

Frank and Joe gasped in surprise. "Is that the one we bought?" Joe burst out.

Aunt Gertrude pursed her lips and looked proud. "Indeed it is," she said. "I put it all together myself. And I might add it's a rare antique you two found!"

When the claps and cheers died down, Frank Hardy spoke up. "Then you *are* in favour of our detective work," he said.

Aunt Gertrude's answer could not be heard amid the laughter that followed, nor could the boys foresee that their next big adventure would be *The Secret of Pirates' Hill*.

From Alfred Hitchcock,

Master of Mystery and Suspense—

A thrilling series of detection and adventure. Meet The Three Investigators – Jupiter Jones, Peter Crenshaw and Bob Andrews. Their motto, "We Investigate Anything", leads the boys into some extraordinary situations – even Jupiter's formidable brain-power is sometimes stumped by the bizarre crimes and weird villains they encounter. But with the occasional piece of advice from The Master himself, The Three Investigators solve a whole lot of sensational mysteries.

1. The Secret of Terror Castle
2. The Mystery of the Stuttering Parrot
3. The Mystery of the Whispering Mummy
4. The Mystery of the Green Ghost
5. The Mystery of the Vanishing Treasure
6. The Secret of Skeleton Island
7. The Mystery of the Fiery Eye
8. The Mystery of the Silver Spider
9. The Mystery of the Screaming Clock
10. The Mystery of the Moaning Cave
11. The Mystery of the Talking Skull
12. The Mystery of the Laughing Shadow
13. The Secret of the Crooked Cat
14. The Mystery of the Coughing Dragon
15. The Mystery of the Flaming Footprints
16. The Mystery of the Nervous Lion
17. The Mystery of the Singing Serpent
18. The Mystery of the Shrinking House
19. The Secret of Phantom Lake
20. The Mystery of Monster Mountain
21. The Secret of the Haunted Mirror
22. The Mystery of the Dead Man's Riddle
23. The Mystery of the Invisible Dog
24. The Mystery of Death Trap Mine
25. The Mystery of the Dancing Devil

Armada

CAPTAIN ARMADA

has a whole shipload of exciting books for you

Here are just some of the best-selling titles that Armada has to offer:

- ☒ **The Shore Road Mystery** Franklin W. Dixon 75p
- ☒ **Biggles in the Orient** Captain W. E. Johns 70p
- ☒ **Spy in Space** Patrick Moore 60p
- ☒ **Turpin and Swiftnick** Richard Carpenter 70p
- ☒ **The Mystery of the Singing Serpent** Alfred Hitchcock 75p
- ☒ **The Mystery of the Dead Man's Riddle** Alfred Hitchcock 75p
- ☒ **The Naughtiest Girl Again** Enid Blyton 70p
- ☒ **Sea Witch Comes Home** Malcolm Saville 70p
- ☒ **The Scarlet Slipper Mystery** Carolyn Keene 75p
- ☒ **The Hardy Boys and Nancy Drew Meet Dracula** TV Tie-in 75p

Armadas are available in bookshops and newsagents, but can also be ordered by post.

HOW TO ORDER
ARMADA BOOKS, Cash Sales Dept., GPO Box 29, Douglas, Isle of Man, British Isles. Please send purchase price of book plus postage, as follows:—

     1—4 Books .... 10p per copy
     5 Books or more .... no further charge
     25 Books sent post free within U.K.

Overseas Customers: 12p per copy

NAME (Block letters)

_____

ADDRESS

_____

_____

While every effort is made to keep prices low, it is sometimes necessary to increase prices on short notice. Armada Books reserve the right to show new retail prices on covers which may differ from those previously advertised in the text or elsewhere.